Stone Mad for Music

This publication has received assistance from IRD Duhallow

First published in 1999 by
Marino Books
an imprint of Mercier Press
16 Hume Street Dublin 2
Tel: (01) 6615299; Fax: (01) 6618583
E.mail: books@marino.ie
Trade enquiries to CMD Distribution
55A Spruce Avenue
Stillorgan Industrial Park
Blackrock County Dublin
Tel: (01) 294 2556; Fax: (01) 294 2564
E.mail: cmd@columba.ie

ISBN 1 86023 097 0
10 9 8 7 6 5 4 3 2
A CIP record for this title is available from the British Library

Cover photography by Don Macmonagle
Cover design by SPACE
Printed in Ireland by ColourBooks, Baldoyle Industrial Estate, Dublin 13

Stone Mad for Music

The Sliabh Luachra Story

Donal Hickey

Sliabh Luachra

The General Sliabh Luachra Area

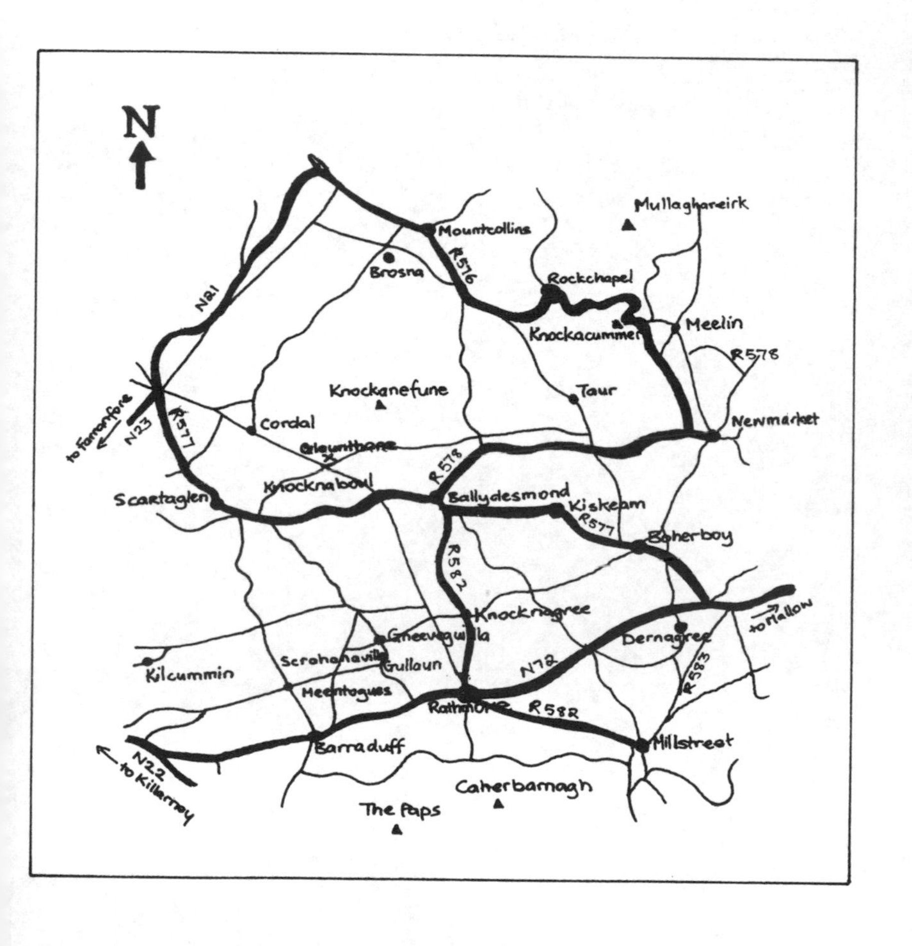

map by Pádraig Ua Duinnín and Mairéad Sheahan

To my wife, Kathleen, and my children,
Tadhg, Aileen and Triona

Acknowledgements

This book has been a long time coming and would never have gone to print without the goodwill and cooperation of many people. Firstly, t here were the people amongst whom I was lucky to grow up around Gneeveguilla, especially those who were old when I was young. I learned a great deal about Sliabh Luachra and its lore from those remarkable people without realising it at the time.

The area is nowadays recognised primarily for its traditional music, but there's more to music than notes and I have attempted to probe the social background and roots of the music and, of course, of the musicians themselves. Neither can the area's poetic tradition be overlooked. Indeed, it could be said that the music and the poetry go hand in hand.

Local history publications such as the *Sliabh Luachra Journal* and *Seanchas Dúthalla* are becoming invaluable reference sources for students of the area and will become even more valuable in the future.

Many people were generous to me with their time and knowledge in the course of research down the years and they are credited throughout the book.

This book is not meant to be a complete record of

all musicians, singers, poets and other artists of Sliabh Luachra. Just because some people are not mentioned does not mean that they are being dismissed in any way. It would not be humanly possible to include everybody.

Thanks to the inimitable Éamon Kelly, who personifies the oral traditions of Sliabh Luachra, for writing the foreword. I am also indebted to journalistic colleagues, in particular Ray Ryan, and to photographers whose work illustrates the book. The cover pictures are by Don MacMonagle and the map is the work of Pádraig Ua Duinnín and Mairéad Sheahan.

Publisher Jo O'Donoghue of Marino Books has been a driving force and a constant source of encouragement. Thanks are also due to IRD Duhallow Ltd for their support and to the Kerry County Library staff, notably those in the Killarney branch library.

Finally, a word of appreciation to my wife, Kathleen, and children, Tadhg, Aileen and Triona, for creating the space to allow me do the work.

Contents

Part II: Music in Words

Foreword by Éamon Kelly

I often say to myself, 'Is Sliabh Luachra a place or a state of mind?' Something of both, I suppose. The exact borders of the territory are never very clear to me. Some say they form a triangle from Millstreet to Killarney with its apex in Castleisland. By the base of the triangle is Cathair Chrobhdhearg, known locally as the City, a place of pilgrimage going back to the time when Homer was a boy.

Rising to the south of the City are *Na Cionna*, the Paps. In Irish these twin mountains of great grandeur are called *An Dá Chích Dannan*, the Breasts of the Goddess Dana. From either summit, I am told, one gets the best view of Sliabh Luachra, a wild landscape of bog and farmland reclaimed from the moor. The *Abhainn Uí Chriadha*, which carried the famous moving bog of a century ago, makes its way to the Flesk, and the white straight-as-a-dye by-road runs from Bealnadeega to Gullane before it turns east to the area's capital, Gneeveguilla.

Donncha Ó Céilleachair in his biography (co-written with Pronsias Ó Conluain) of an tAthair Pádraig Ua Duinnín called the Paps the Olympus of Ireland, where the gods of the old Celts lived. From their front doors the poets Aodhagán Ó Rathaille and Eoghan Rua Ó Súilleabháin saw these mountains each morning as they rose to sniff the air, and they were ever their inspiration.

I heard an old man say that before the Elizabethan plantations Sliabh Luachra was a wilderness. Men who had been deprived of their rich Munster lands found shelter within the triangle and wrenched a place to live from the moorland.

All my people had their roots in Sliabh Luachra, and when my Auntie Bridgie sat down to trace relationships it seemed to us children that we were connected by blood to a great many people in that place.

Later when we lived at Carrigeen in Glenflesk my mother would send me at the age of ten to walk all the way to Gullane with news of our well-being for my grandfather and grandmother. From our house to theirs was a tidy step, and even in the daylight I was fearful passing Béalnadeaga because of a story my mother told us about that crossroads. A spirit used to appear there at the dead of night and men out late were frightened to death by her. She had the power to drag a man from a galloping horse, and was said to blind her victim by squirting her breast-milk into his eyes.

Priests came to bless the place where she haunted, but the spirit remained until a holy friar in a brown habit read over the spot. His reading of Latin was effective. He banished the spirit to the Dead Sea and the sentence he pronounced on her was that she should drain its waters with a silver spoon for all eternity.

During these visits to Gullane I remember meeting Charlie O'Leary, the last Irish speaker of Sliabh Luachra. When I was older and able to understand Irish he said to me, '*Duine de mhuintir Chíosáin tusa.*'

'I am not,' I said. 'My name is Kelly.'

'Then your mother was a Kissane,' he persisted.

'No,' I told him, 'her name was Cashman.'

'Ah, that explains it,' he said. 'The first man of your mother's name to come to these quarters to rent a bit of land was asked by Lord Kenmare's agent, "What is your name?" "*Tadhg Ó Cíosáin,*" the man answered. "I am tired of unpronounceable and unwritable names," said the agent. "From now on you are Cashman." The new name went down in the book and my ancestor lost his Gaelic nomenclature.

Donncha Ó Céilleachair, who interviewed Charlie O'Leary when he was researching the book on Father Dineen, told me that Charlie could recite Eoghan Rua's verse and, unusually, he had an air to each poem to which he sang the lines.

Though the neighbouring men sitting around my father's fire when I was small knew no Irish they had a wealth of stories about Eoghan Rua. It seems he was one day going to Cork and outside Millstreet a school-master picked up something from the road and said to Eoghan, 'Look at that, I am in luck for the day – I found a horseshoe.'

'No doubt,' Eoghan remarked, 'education is a

wonderful thing. I wouldn't know whether that was a horseshoe or a mare's shoe.'

The parish priest calling out the names of those who hadn't paid their dues enquired, 'Where is Eoghan Ó Súilleabháin?' Eoghan answered and the priest asked, 'Are you Eoghan a' Dirrín?' '*Ní mé*,' arsa Eoghan, '*ach Eoghan a' bhéil bhinn*.'

Sweet, melodious and eloquent was Eoghan's voice, and those characteristics are evident today when a Gneeveguilla man or woman gets up to sing. And men still follow Eoghan's trade of making noise. When I was young we looked forward on Saturday to the *Cork Weekly Examiner* for the songs of my mother's cousin, the Bard of Knocknagree, one Ned Owen Buckley.

Snatches of a ballad I recall which lamented the passing of an aged neighbour. After more than a modicum of praise for the departed soul, each verse ended with the line, 'But he wasn't long going in the end.'

Nowadays at the mention of Sliabhh Luachra we think of music and song, storytelling and dancing. The music of Denis Murphy – that divine fiddler – is in the archives of RTÉ, and every time I hear it my feet itch for the flagged kitchen floor from which we knocked sparks when I was growing up. My friend and relative Johnny O'Leary played the button accordeon and accompanied Denis Murphy's fiddle. Johnny is among those who carry on the tradition.

Sliabh Luachra features in the stories of Fionn Mac

Cumhail's time that tradition has handed down to us. It was from there that Bodach an Chóta Lachtna, that great big ugly laughing clown, set out to race the Greek hero Caol an Iarainn, all the way to the Hill of Howth.

Sliabh Luachra is as vital today as it ever was. Long may it be so, whether it is a state of mind or a mystic moorland defined by an isosceles triangle.

Part 1

Words and Music

1

Sliabh Luachra – A Place Apart

The haunting Irish word, *draíocht*, has been used to define the aura or atmosphere in Sliabh Luachra when traditional music is being played at its best and most authentic. In English, *draíocht* means magic or enchantment, but words cannot fully describe something that reaches into the soul: depending on the occasion, it could be a feeling of exultation or deep sorrow evoked, for example, by the playing of a slow air.

Draíocht is a spiritual experience that's not always found at a fleadh cheoil or in a crowded pub. Exceptional musicians – the late Pádraig O'Keeffe and Denis Murphy being prime examples – can generate it. *Draíocht* touches the emotions and is much more likely in intimate settings when a remarkably gifted musician plays for himself, with a few others, or for a few friends.

And there are those who are convinced that babies as young as six months can respond to the rhythm of the music which is known for its vibrancy and get-up-and-dance feeling.

If music is the mystical power in the area, it is

complemented in the natural environment by a horseshoe of mountains of varying shapes and sizes that cradle Sliabh Luachra. Of these mountains, twins, known as the Paps, are by far the most striking. It's easy enough to understand how the first people who came into Sliabh Luachra thousands of years ago could have been so awestruck by the identical Paps that they began to treat them as a deity.

Ancient people have left their marks scattered around the area – standing stones, cairns, fulachta fiadh and non-descript mounds are in the fields and sometimes half-hidden in the vivid yellow furze that lights up the land in springtime.

The Paps preside over all these antiquities. Shaped like the female breast, they were dedicated by the pagan settlers to Dana, mother goddess of the Tuatha Dé Dannan. Lying five miles south-west of Rathmore, the Paps are the work of nature, but the nipples (two cairns of stone on top) were built by man. At the base of the Paps is a famous stone ring fort, called Cahercrobdarrig, a place of pagan worship which is known locally as the City.

The ascent of the Paps is not too difficult, taking about an hour, and is well worth the effort. On a clear day climbers are rewarded by panoramic views as far as Kerry Head to the north; Killarney, Slea Head and the Atlantic to the West; the Galtee mountains to the east and Kenmare to the south.

Sliabh Luachra (rushy mountain) is not a clearly defined geographical area but a bleak and wet stretch of countryside best known for its treasures of traditional music and poetry. The area has its own beauty – nothing like the so-called Heaven's Reflex or manicured refinement of nearby Killarney, but something more primeval – bracken, gorse, foxglove, buttercups, birch, hazel, peat, marshes, an endless maze of bohereens, farms reclaimed from the moorland, patchworks of cultivated fields and heather-scented uplands. Poets drew inspiration from seeing the sun rise over Clara and from the lengthening shadows that glide over Caherbarnagh on summer evenings.

It's a landscape that changes as you move from one townland to the next and grows on those who know it. Anyone who ever drank bog 'tay' or heard the trill of the lark and curlew in clear skies over shiny banks of turf will understand: nor could you forget the peace and contentment of being soothed by gentle summer breezes in wild, elevated places like Meenganine where the infant Blackwater gurgles forth in a trickle that soon becomes a mighty river flowing a hundred miles to the sea at Youghal.

Like almost everything else on the landscape, the Blackwater, which divides Cork and Kerry, has inspired verse. In local pubs the late Ballydesmond postman, singer and yarn-spinner, Timmy Curney O'Sullivan, used to recite:

It rushes forth with its incarnation,
Through rocky cascades it rushes down
And ceases not its agitation
'Till it reaches King Williamstown

Sliabh Luachra was once in the ancient barony of Maguinhy and, in today's terms, the area embraces a large part of east Kerry, north-west Cork and some of west Limerick. The are no lines on a map to show its boundaries and some people, including the writer Con Houlihan, have described it as a cultural enclave or moveable feast, and not so much a physical territory. There are nevertheless geological characteristics – not to speak of the ever-present rushes – which can be used to define the area.

Loosely outlined, the area is bordered by the towns of Killarney, Castleisland, Abbeyfeale, Newmarket and by the Paps. Some would argue that such a description is too wide and would say that the truc Sliabh Luachra is centred around the core area of Gneeveguilla (due to its close association with the poets), Rathmore, Knocknagree, Ballydesmond and Scartaglen. Musically, however it is broader than that.

Critical in terms of definition are physical factors. For a start, the land in east Kerry, north-west Cork and the adjoining area of west Limerick is practically the same. The land is floored by a rock series which is sometimes called coal measures, while the soil cover is generally a glacial drift – a wet mineral clay with sizeable portions of peat.[1]

Coal has been mined in areas bordering Sliabh Luachra, particularly in Duhallow. Beneath the coal measures can be found a rock floor of carboniferous limestone, while another common rock is shale, known locally as 'pencil'. Shale doesn't allow for easy soakage, which partly explains the reason for poor natural drainage in an area which has pretty high rainfall of up to sixty inches per annum.

Sliabh is the Gaelic word for mountain, but when Sliabh Luachra people use the word 'mountain' they often mean rising bogland, or coarse, rough country: not mountains within the generally accepted meaning of the term.

Sources dating to the middle of the 18th century also refer to the nature of the landscape when describing the area. 'The eastern parts adjoining to the County of Cork are coarse and mountainous; and besides the mountains of Slievelogher [sic], which in the reign of Queen Elizabeth 1, were deemed impassable, as the writer of Pacata Hibernia informs us, it comprehends also the territory called Glanflesk [sic] which has been of late years much improved, enclosed and cultivated . . . '[2] (Queen Elizabeth 1 reigned from 1558 to 1603.)

Going much further back in time, there are references in the *Fiannaíocht* to Luachair, Teamhair Luachra and Sliabh Luachra, which is rather flatteringly described as '*Sliabh leathanmhór, lánaoibhinn*' [a broad expanse of mountain, full of beauty].

The first people came to the area thousands of years before the birth of Christ. There is ample evidence to show that the southern half, under the Paps, was populated in early times and, much later, the wider inhospitable landscape became a refuge for those in flight from the authorities.

Local historians are virtually unanimously of the view that the pre-Christian people who were enraptured by the beauty and contours of the Paps dedicated the twin mountains to the goddess Dana or Anu. Primitive people saw in the Paps a reflection of the gods and, in the shadow of the mountains, built a place of worship, the City, which survives in good condition.

A highly respected expert on the oral traditions of the City is Dan Cronin, who has spent a lifetime probing the history and the folklore of the area. The city was a place of pagan worship and has religious connections to this day. It is now very much under Christian influence with a statue of the Blessed Virgin incongruously standing out in the old pagan and druidic stronghold.

Dan Cronin describes it as 'one of the most ancient, historical and interesting religious sites not only in Ireland but in the entire western world'[3].

The city is made up of a circular dry stone wall, ten feet high and six feet thick. Its diameter is about 150 feet. At one time, there was a large stone circle in the centre, which bore traces of ogham writing, and a number of beehive cells. People lived within the City up to the mid-1980s. Outside the western wall is a holy well. According to local historians, the original well inside the walls was destroyed by land agents in the area, the Cronins, around 1800.

Historically, the City has been associated with human sacrifice and local townlands to this day have names such as Gortdearg (red field) and Gortnagceann (field of the heads). When paganism and druidism had run their course Christianity took over, most likely at the time of St Cuimin (589-661AD). But the old pre-Christian festival of Bealtaine still survives, with people making 'rounds' on May Day, which was, in living memory, a local pattern day and an occasion of great merriment, with music, song and dance. Water was taken from the holy well and prayers said for healthy animals and bountiful crops.

Some interesting research is currently being carried out by the Newmarket archaeologist Raymond O'Sullivan, who is undertaking an environmental project in western Duhallow, the County Cork side of Sliabh Luachra. His focus is on ring barrows – earthen mounds fashioned like fried eggs and surrounded by an outer bank. The ring barrows, which date from the mid-Bronze Age, around 1500BC, were used for human burials and are evidence of what O'Sullivan theorises may be the first major colonisation of the area.

For all the world like mini ring forts, the ring barrows are mainly to be found in the upland countryside between Tullylease and Gneeveguilla. The biggest concentration is in the Kiskeam–Cullen area along the banks of the River Araglen and they run in a line that could be described as a local version of the Valley of the Kings.

Sliabh Luachra is also peppered with ring forts, which were farmsteads in the period 500-1000AD. There was a substantial influx much later when some people dispossessed in the Plantation of Laois and Offaly (1558) fled south to the bogs and rushes of east Kerry – many of them O'Connors, a common name in the district today. However, it was after the battles of Kinsale (1601) and Cnoc na nOs (1647) that most of the people arrived. For landless, poverty-stricken, fleeing people the rushes and swamps offered a safe haven. Remoteness was another attraction. At the time, roads linking Tralee and Killarney with Cork had not been constructed and Gaelic traditions found a sanctuary.

After the defeat of the Earl of Desmond, a major landmark in Munster, in the rebellion of 1579–80, and the demise of the big houses there came utter depredation, and ordinary people suffered great misery and hardship during the 17th and 18th centuries. They became even more isolated. The outside world closed on them and they turned to the intimate arts of music and poetry. Into this environment were born the famous poets, Aodhagán Ó Rathaille and Eoghan Rua Ó Súilleabháin. Their verse and the old music helped to sustain the spirit of the people in such difficult times.

Tháinigh meath ar an Ghaeilge sa cheanntar taréis an Ghorta. Ag an am san, bhí an teanga á labhairt go forleathan i Sliabh Luachra. De réir mhóráireamh 1851, bhí 25,598 cainteoirí Gaeilge in mBarúntacht Mhágh gCoinche (68.5%) agus Gaeilge amháin a bhí ag 4,000 díobh. Sa bhliain 1891, ní raibh ach 7,432 Gaeilgeoirí (28.3%). Tá an Ghaeilge imithe mar theanga labhartha i

Sliabh Luachra anois ach maireann an ceol agus an rince Gaelach go beo bríomhar. [The Irish language started to decline in the district after the Famine – from 25,598 Irish speakers in Maguinihy in 1851 to 7,432 in 1891.]

Few areas have been as romanticised, nearly always by outsiders. But life in times past was far from easy for the people who lived there and they didn't, of course, spend all their time playing music, dancing polka sets or writing poetry. When their daily task of wrenching a living from the land was done, their culture provided them with wholesome enjoyment and a creative outlet for the more artistic amongst them: something that lifted them all above the humdrum.

2

The Origins of the Music and Dance

Much of what is today regarded as traditional Irish music and dance is not really that traditional at all and not nearly as ancient as some people might think: indeed, it is quite modern and only a few hundred years old.

Some of our music, especially reels, is Scottish in origin and the polka set is an import from France which dancing masters adapted to suit existing tunes here. Be that as it may, however, we now have created a widely accepted brand of folk music and dance with a distinct Irish flavour, Sliabh Luachra having its own regional variation. Irish traditional music has similarities with that found in other parts of the world, especially in mountainous and prairie areas in America where Scottish, English and French people settled and brought their own culture with them.

There were long spells in our recent history when Irish culture and all that it encompassed were despised by a sizeable number of people. Like the period after the Famine, when the Irish people turned against their native language, there was a barren period between the early 1920s, after the Civil War, and the 1960s, when people tended to turn their backs on Irish music and musicians. We also had the ridiculous spectacle of clergy trying to outlaw dances, apparently on grounds that they threatened the 'morals' of young people.

When the so-called respectability deserted the music in those bleak times, it was kept alive by dedicated little groups in scattered rural areas, in some of the poorer parts of our cities and by travellers. A case of marginalised people preserving something that was also pushed to the margins.

That's all hard to understand now as we face into the new millennium when Irish music is at an all-time high in terms of popularity. However, we need only go back a generation to find musicians – who, were they alive today, would be in the superstar league – dying penniless and appreciated only by a faithful few. Sliabh Luachra's Pádraig O'Keeffe, who got no material rewards and nothing like the recognition he deserved in his own lifetime, is a typical example.

In attempting to go back in time in Sliabh Luachra, we have to rely largely on the oral tradition, a notable exception being the work of the scholar-priest, an tAthair Pádraig Ua Duinnín, who researched and wrote about the life and work of the major poets. He was born in 1860, 76 years after the death of the renowned Sliabh Luachra poet and folk hero, Eoghan Rua Ó Súilleabháin, and would, therefore, have some reliable knowledge from tradition of what happened in the previous couple of centuries.

He tells us that on Sunday evenings throughout the summer season, a 'patron', or dancing festival, was held at Faha and, in the plain beneath, a vigorous hurling match was carried on. The time referred to by an t-Athair Ua Duinnín was the second half of the 18th century when Eoghan Rua Ó Súilleabháin, was in his prime.

Faha, near the western bank of the Owenacree river on the most direct road between Gneeveguilla and Killarney, is now known as Annagh, and a memorial has been erected to the seat of learning, music, jollity and poetry that once flourished there. Eoghan Rua lived a short distance away at Meentogues and along with another man from the locality, Aodhagán Ó Rathaille, ranks amongst the most celebrated poets in Gaelic literature. A famous court of poetry assembled there in Eoghan's time. Music and dance were an essential part of the scene and even if the poets have long since vanished the music lives on.

Traditional music has tended to thrive in areas like Sliabh Luachra, where holdings are modest and the land unyielding. A view held by some observers is that bad land produces good music. In such areas long ago people were close-knit, sharing what they had and helping each other in order to survive. There is a theory that folk music is the poetry of the people – an expression of their ups and downs. Their recreation was simple and they provided their own entertainment, passing on the culture to succeeding generations.

Importantly, there was a story behind every tune, song and dance, as their titles generally indicate. Take for instance, a polka known as 'Who Spilt The Po?' which the late Jack Connell, of Lighthouse, Ballydesmond, used to play. A man went to the village one day to bring home draught stout – long before six-packs or alcohol in cans were heard of. The man forgot to take the usual earthen ware jar with him for the stout, but his wife had bought a new po (chamber pot) that day so he decided to take home the precious brew in the po.

But, as a ditty goes, things didn't work out too well for 'the road it was rough, the donkey was tough and that's how I spilt the po.'

How old the music is we cannot say with absolute accuracy: some scholars would argue that its roots are deep in the old Gaelic world and that it is reasonable to expect that some of the music of ancient times was assimilated into the evolving newer music. The music has developed with each generation contributing something and all the time maintaining continuity.

Much of the Sliabh Luachra music is unwritten in the strict sense and that which can be traced was written in the first half of the 18th century. Some of the tunes have their origin in lilting, or dydling (puss music) and various performers have added their own touches down the line with the better tunes surviving and becoming part of the repertoire.

The music is closely linked to places and personalities. There are tunes with names such as 'The Kilcummin Slide', 'The Glounthane Frolics', 'Jimmy Doyle's Polka' and 'O'Keeffe's Dream'. Musicians usually say where and from whom they get their tunes, again underlining the importance of the music being handed on.

A leading west Limerick musician and music scholar, Dónal de Barra, who was president of Comhaltas Ceoltóirí Éireann (CCÉ) on two occasions, describes Sliabh Luachra music as 'simple and straightforward, but its ornamentation, rhythm and sheer life set it apart. It is epitomised by what might be called soul – the heart and feeling that comes through the music. It is essentially dance music, with musicians and dancers synchronising and bringing the best out of each other.'[1]

The style, he adds, has been created by strong characters, many of whom were also teachers who had a powerful influence on their pupils. By such means the style was preserved and passed on. The most famous teacher in recent times was the late Pádraig O'Keeffe, who inherited music from the last century and passed it on.

Teachers such as O'Keeffe have been described by broadcaster and collector Seán Mac Réamoinn as the 'scattered Fellows of an unendowed, unhoused and unrecognised Academy of Irish Music and tradition for perhaps two hundred years'.

As far as Sliabh Luachra is concerned another key

factor in the preservation of the music was the relative isolation of the area in times past. It became a refuge for native Irish people who had been driven out of their lands in other parts of the country in what would nowadays be referred to as ethnic cleansing. Hardship was the sad lot of such people who turned to the intimate arts of music and poetry as they became cut off from the outside world.

A turnpike road between Cork and Listowel was built in the middle of the 18th century and it took in part of Sliabh Luachra, going through Millstreet, Shinnagh, Knocknaboul Cross and Castleisland. But many of the roads used today were not built until the 1820s and 1830s. A key figure at that time was geologist and civil engineer Richard Griffith who supervised a public works programme. The programme was confined to areas where there were no roads fit for wheeled carriages.

According to folk tradition, Gneeveguilla alone had up to twenty fiddlers before the Famine.[2] Dancing teachers moved from house to house. Pattern days and fairs in places like Knocknagree, Millstreet and Castle-island provided an outlet for musicians who enlivened the atmosphere.

Polka sets are now the most popular traditional dances in Sliabh Luachra. Jig sets, in vogue prior to World War I, have been undergoing a revival, offering dancers welcome variety. But the set – meaning a set of quadrilles – is not Irish in origin and is believed to have originated in France, spreading to other parts of

Europe over two hundred years ago. The Sliabh Luachra set comprises six figures, finishing with a slide and a hornpipe, and lasts about thirty minutes. Four energetic couples take the floor and there are few more effective ways of burning up calories. In confined spaces, a half-set with two couples can be danced.

According to an acknowledged authority, the late Breandán Breathnach, many Irish dances originated in England.[3] Solo, or step dances – jigs, reels and hornpipes – became common in the last part of the 18th century, thanks mainly to the work of dancing teachers. Sets became popular in the 19th century. The sets were brought to Ireland and England by soldiers in the British army. Here in Ireland dancing masters adapted these dances to local styles putting in native steps for ballroom steps and quickening the pace to keep time with jigs and reels. In that way, sets became part of the Irish scene and spread all over the country.

Some tunes which have long since been part of the scene in Sliabh Luachra came from the other side of the Irish Sea. Reels like 'Lord MacDonald' and 'Miss MacLeod' were at first Scottish, but were naturalised here. Many jigs, however, are believed to be Irish in origin and the same can be said for slow airs.

There was no shortage of music teachers who drifted from place to place checking on pupils' progress at regular intervals. Dancing was a hugely popular social pastime and musicians were always in demand. Some of the teachers-musicians were blind or disabled in other ways, and music offered them a means of earning a living.

Not much is known about most of the teachers, but they live on in memory. A travelling music teacher who was known only as Graddy (probably O'Grady) is credited with bringing music into Rockchapel, County Cork, on the eastern side of Sliabh Luachra. Most likely he came from County Limerick and in his younger days is said to have played in the big houses. Legend has it that one of the landed class for whom he played was so impressed that he took Graddy to play for the king and queen of England in Buckingham Palace. This didn't go down too well with nationally-minded people in his own place and he fled to the hilly fastness of 'The Rock' (Rockchapel) where he stayed with different families for many years. Graddy died some time in the 1840s and is mentioned in old, local songs. In more recent times a character, Daniel 'Saucepan' Hartnett, taught music in that area.

James Gandsey, 'the Killarney Minstrel', is another who survives in folk memory, though he died in 1857 at 90 years of age. A smallpox attack in his infancy left Gandsey almost blind, but that didn't take from his musical ability. His father was a soldier in Ross Castle and his mother was a native of Killarney. Gandsey was also known as Lord Headley's Piper and some of his tunes, including 'Jackson's Morning Brush', 'The Fox Chase' and 'Madame Bonaparte', are in the general Sliabh Luachra repertoire. Gandsey was buried in

Muckross Abbey, Killarney, and a plaque has been erected to his memory.

In the old days, some of the instruments were home-made; *sean-nós* singer Jimmy O'Brien remembers seeing his uncle, Paddy Coakley, of Lyreatough, making a flute from the branch of an alder tree. The centre of the branch was scooped out and Paddy then reddened six-inch nails to make holes for fingers. The end product may not have been concert pitch, but it still made music.

A neighbour, Andrew Owen McCarthy, made a fiddle with wood from a tea chest and used ordinary timber for the neck of the instrument. It was a strange contraption, but again music came from it. A hair comb with paper around it could also make music when held between the lips and blown into.

Traditionally, the fiddle has been the most popular instrument in Sliabh Luachra and the pipes were also played there in the 19th century: Gandsey wasn't short of company. In the first quarter of the 20th century, however, the melodeon and, later, the accordeon began to make inroads at the expense of the fiddle, whilst the ever-faithful and cheap tin whistle has always been common in the area. Friends or relatives in America sent home melodeons, or the purchase price of same. The instrument caught on and was very quickly adapted to Irish music.

Before long there was a melodeon in every house. Youngsters were tempted to try their hands at the melodeon and they found it easier to squeeze notes from it than they would, say, from a fiddle. Some taught themselves to play the melodeon. Another advantage was that the melodeon, with a relatively simple rhythm, suited set dancing and could be heard clearly by large numbers of people prior to the coming of electronic amplification. The melodeon was also very suitable for waltzes and modern dances which came in with the dance hall era in the 1920s and '30s.

The concertina was favoured by some traditional musicians, generally women, but never attained the degree of popularity in Sliabh Luachra as it did, for instance, in Clare. In the past forty years, the accordeon has taken over from the melodeon and is now the most popular instrument.

In the 19th century, dancing was done mainly in people's homes and at open-air, crossroads platforms in summertime. Several platforms continued to function into the 20th century. They generally operated on Sunday afternoons. One of those still remembered was a timber-floored platform at Tureenglanhee, Knocknagree, run by Maurice Manley, a tailor, musician and music teacher. Maurice himself played the fiddle, accompanied by other musicians. His daughter, Julia, played in later years at Vaughan's hall, Ballydesmond. Another platform was at Newquarter bridge which spans the Blackwater between Gneeveguilla and Ballydesmond.

3

Fresh Air, Easy Minds and Long Lives

In the 1960s Sliabh Luachra hit the headlines for reasons other than its music, although music was almost certainly a factor in the whole story.

An eminent Irish-American pathologist, Dr Albert E. Casey, whose forebears came from Knocknagree, carried out research which showed that Sliabh Luachra people had one of the longest and healthiest lifespans of any community in Ireland, if not in the world. And all this despite having a diet which consisted of plenty of milk, fat bacon, butter, eggs and copious pints of creamy porter for the men. Contrary to the usual trend, the men of Sliabh Luachra were outliving the women by an average of two-and-a-half years.

In a paper to the learned International Academy of Pathology in San Francisco, Dr Casey concluded that the reason was that the menfolk had peace of mind and didn't suffer from too much stress. They were actually living to an average of seventy-seven years, ten years longer than men in US industrial centres.

And why, you might wonder, weren't they all getting heart attacks and dying young from consuming so much cholesterol? Dr Casey didn't provide any medical reasons, but down-to-earth locals would surmise that hard work in the bogs, drains and fields, not to mention set dancing, burnt off the fat very quickly. Fresh air and the closeness of the bogs, which are noted for their preservative powers, were also being cited as reasons for longevity. Dick Hogan, an *Irish Times* journalist with more than a passing interest in Sliabh Luachra, once suggested that a fortune awaited an enterprising person who could devise a way of bottling the fresh, unpolluted upland air.

The men of the area also took their dead ease when it came to getting married. They regarded forty as a reasonable age at which to take a bride and, well before they reached a decision of such moment, negotiations were held to make sure the future union was based on sound business deals involving land and dowries, often brokered by a matchmaker.

The overwhelming majority of such partnerships lasted for life and generally produced many offspring. That's not to say that all marriages were made in heaven. It was very much a man's world: feminism hadn't yet gripped the land. Most women didn't have careers outside the home, or independent financial means, apart maybe from selling eggs, or fattening a few turkeys and geese for the Christmas market. Separation, not to mention divorce, was frowned on socially and also by the powerful Catholic Church. Some women had tough, miserable lives and their personal needs were sacrificed for the sake of other people. It wasn't easy to get out of a bad match and women so affected generally decided to put up with their lot: they didn't have much choice.

A generation or two ago, women worked in the fields, milked cows, fed pigs and did all sorts of manual labour as well as looking after their homes. Rearing large families – giving birth to a child a year in certain cases – they didn't have much time for a social life and they never set foot inside the door of a pub. But change has occurred very rapidly and the women of yesteryear wouldn't know the lifestyle of their successors if they returned. Indeed, if we're to believe all that's said about them, such women were pure saints and spent a lot of their time on their knees praying – with the odd exception.

It may have been a male-dominated world, but some Sliabh Luachra women were remarkable achievers in business and in humanitarian and caring ways. Women like the late Minnie Barry and Maria Kate Moynihan, who was an invalid, built up highly successful shops in Gneeveguilla in bad times. And they were just two examples. There were countless unsung heroines such as nurses, struggling widows with large young families to rear and women who unselfishly set their own personal development aside to care for aged or disabled relatives.

But back to Dr Casey. His findings attracted researchers from other countries and Sliabh Luachra people found themselves being compared with the centenarians of the Andes, South American Indians and groups of Russians, Arabs and Chinese as having the secrets of a long and healthy life.

Ray Ryan, a veteran journalist with the *Examiner* who writes wonderfully about his native Sliabh Luachra, interviewed some of the old people at the time, including Tom Jim Healy, of Knocknaboul, Ballydesmond, who symbolised the story and became a media personality in the process. Tom was then ninety-one but more often than not he was to be found in the bog cutting turf when media people called to see him.

When asked if he and his contemporaries ever worried, he replied in a flash:

> Not on your life. Our only trouble was to find out where was the next pattern or house dance. They were jolly times and the people were much more sociable and loyal. This coupled with hard work and plain food kept them alive. We used to dance 'The Jenny Lind' and 'The Walls of Limerick' at weddings and patterns. All they have nowadays is this jig-jog of a foreign dance which shouldn't be allowed at all![1]

Tom, a tall, sprightly man who never weighed more than eleven stone, caused further astonishment when he declared that he took no notice of walking the eight miles from his home to Castleisland and back again the same day, even in his old age. He was just six months short of his hundredth birthday when he died.

Dr Casey was known internationally for his cancer research, but his legacy to Sliabh Luachra consists of fifteen volumes of historical material relating to the Cork–Kerry area under the title *O'Kief, Coshe Mang, Slieve Lougher and the Upper Blackwater in Ireland.*[2] Dr Casey was aged seventy-nine when he died in Birmingham, Alabama, USA, in December 1982.

It would be easy to portray an idyllic, pastoral way of life in Sliabh Luachra, full of music and carefree pleasure. Truth is that life was difficult in the old days for the great majority of people who had to eke out an existence from rugged, uncompromising terrain. They saw sons and daughters emigrate in droves to England and America – in the middle of the 19th century there was even planned emigration from Ballydesmond. Many of those who left never returned.

The people had very little money, but entertained themselves with their own music, which gave expression to their joys and sorrows and escape from the drudgery of daily toil. Music and poetry – and most importantly the rare personalities who were musicians and poets – helped keep the spirit of the people alive.

Neither was laughter too far from the surface and the witty man or woman has always been treasured. Every day you'll hear yarns spun by such people, like the one about the man being given his breakfast by a neighbour before heading to the bog with the man of the house. 'How do you like your egg, Denny, hard or soft?' she inquired. 'Boiled with another one,' came the instant reply.

And there was the old man who got tired of listening to a woman boasting about the wonders of a new turf-burning range at a time when the wondrous product was first making its appearance in the area. 'We don't burn half the turf since we got it,' she declared. 'Well why don't ye got a second one so? Ye'd burn no turf at all then,' he retorted.

There's a strong tradition concerning a host of folk cures, both animal and human. The area had charm-setters and people reputed to have the gift of healing. A popular cure for worms in calves was known as *cleas na péiste*. This involved putting nine knots on a string and then ripping the knots one by one, hitting the calf on its back with the string each time.

Home-dispensed medicine obviated the need for visits to the nearest pharmacy, which could be many miles away. A concoction for curing burns, for instance, included a glass of linseed oil, a glass of lime water and a glass of cream. All were mixed into a bottle until the cream got good and thick. The prescription was then rubbed on to the burn and some sufferers swore they got relief from it.

Pisheogs (evil spells) were worked in the area, usually by malicious people wishing to draw some evil on their neighbours. People lived in genuine fear of pisheogs and the finding of eggs, dead animals or entrails on one's land was sometimes interpreted as an indication that somebody was wishing you bad luck. Some rare instances of pisheogs were reported up to the 1960s, but the practice appears to have died out.

The area has had to endure its share of tragedies, one of the most notable being the death of ten people in a flood that rushed through Clydagh Valley, lying in the shadows of the Paps, in August 1831. Without warning and in broad daylight the valley floor was covered by what was described as a roaring torrent, three hundred yards wide and 16 feet deep, which took everything before it including a baby whose cradle floated for two miles on the water before overturning. The baby then drowned.

Houses, cattle and crops were destroyed in the cloud-burst and severe distress was caused to landowners, who received no help or compensation from the government or landlords.[3]

The Famine also took its toll in Sliabh Luachra, reflected in a substantial fall in population, as shown by the census figures of 1851, and an exodus to workhouses in Castleisland, Killarney, Millstreet, Mallow and other surrounding towns. There isn't a large volume of oral tradition regarding the horrors of the Famine in the region – it was obviously a time people preferred to forget – but some written accounts give an insight into what they suffered. The Knocknagree poet, Ned Buckley, poignantly told of how two men died of hunger in Knocknagree. One of the men had brought the corpses of his two children in a bag from Ballydesmond to be buried in Nohoval cemetery, six miles from his home. Having laid his children to rest, he himself died of hunger and exhaustion on the return journey. Other heartbreaking stories tell of how people tried to survive by eating grass and weeds during those terrible times.

A notable tragedy was the moving bog disaster of Christmas 1896 in which the Donnelly family – father, mother and six of their children – were all swept away as they slept peacefully in their cottage near Gneeveguilla. The landslide resulted in a massive amount of bog floating down the valley of the Owenacree river, with some of the material ending up in the Lakes of Killarney, fourteen miles away.[4]

One of the Donnelly children, Katie, who was aged thirteen at the time, survived because she was staying with relatives, several miles away. She later married, returned to the site of her old home and brought up her family there. Katie (Mrs O'Donoghue) died in 1964, aged 81, and was buried in Gneeveguilla.

Sliabh Luachra has a strong religious tradition, which is practically 100 per cent Catholic in the core area. An obvious historic reason for this is that the land, because of its poor quality, didn't attract British settlers and planters, who would have been chiefly Protestant. Very welcome settlers, albeit for only a short time, were the Cistercian monks who, having been uprooted from their base in France, came to Rathmore in 1831 and opened a monastery on the site of the presbytery before moving to Mount Melleray, County Waterford, in 1837. The monks were accepted graciously in Rathmore and, according to local folk tradition, the high number of vocations to the priesthood and religious life from Rathmore parish was a gesture of divine thanksgiving for the hospitality shown to the monks.[5]

What appears to have been a most successful mission was held in Rathmore in 1898, and the Redemptorist priests who conducted the mission reported afterwards that there wasn't one Protestant in the parish of about 8,000 souls.

The land war was also fought in Sliabh Luachra; the Whiteboys, Moonlighters and other agrarian groups were being active, and some significant ambushes were staged there during the War of Independence. It was against a background of general unrest that the GAA, founded in 1884, took early root in the area, with the Rathmore club being affiliated in 1888. The GAA has since been the predominant sporting organisation on both sides of the River Blackwater. There are clubs in every parish, all well equipped with pitches and facilities and steeped in their own histories. Clubs also provide facilities for general enjoyment and command intense loyalty. Gaelic football is by far the most popular game. Handball is also played, whilst hurling is largely confined to the Cork side of Sliabh Luachra.

In common with what took place in many other parts of the country, Irish as a spoken language went into rapid decline in Sliabh Luachra and neighbouring Duhallow in the second half of the 19th century. This is illustrated by a story of how a priest posted to Rathmore around 1850 had to deliver his sermons in Irish so as to be understood by his flock. Forty years later, however, he had to preach in English for the same reason.

People like Donnchadh Ó Rinn of Ballydesmond worked valiantly *ar son na Gaeilge* in the early years of the century – work which was continued by another member of his family, also Donnchadh – but there was no stopping the encroachment of English, a development that was helped by, among other factors, the educational policies of the day.

Some native speakers survived into the 20th century and more than a half-dozen people in Gneeveguilla officially described themselves as native speakers in the 1930s, with Charlie O'Leary of Gullane being a renowned scholar and Gaeilgeoir.

Cullen is a place where efforts are still being made to revive and preserve an *teanga*. Today, some people regard Cullen as a mini-Gaeltacht and it has won several Glór na nGael competitions with Gaeilgeoir Pádraig Ó hIcheadha to the fore.

English is spoken with an Irish blas to this day in Sliabh Luachra Even the phraseology is very close to Irish and many Irish words are part of the English spoken by the people every day. You might call a fellow an *amadán* (clown) if he wasn't *slachtmhar* (tidy) around the house, even though he might be full of *teasbach* (exceptionally lively) in taking cattle to the *glaise* (stream). A *meitheal* (group) of men would be most useful in the bog, but there might not be much *meas* (regard) on people less skilled in such work. Sometimes in the bog you'd meet fine *grámhar* (pleasant) people, while others would be full of *ráiméis* (nonsense) and you would be inclined to throw *caoráns* (small sods) at them, or give them a *sceilp* (slap) with your *ciotóg* (left hand).

This is just a sample of Irish words that have become part of the English vernacular.

Placenames are also redolent of the old Gaelic and their everyday pronounciation has not suffered as much from the English bastardisation of placenames as those of many other places. For instance, the townland of Maughantourig (summer grazing area for cattle) is still pronounced as if in Gaelic as is Meenagisheach (marsh with makeshift bridge).

Even though the language has disappeared, other aspects of Gaelic culture continue to thrive. A few local songs in Irish have survived and a house dance in Caher-barnagh, not far from Cullen, around the year 1900, was the subject of a song called 'The Caher Porter Ball'. It is typical of the songs that were composed about local events at the time. The following two verses feature the names of publicans, characters and dances:

Na hasail bheannaithe agus cros na naomh orthu,
Ag tarraingt an porter gan collar nó hames orthu,
Bhí porter Willie Hassett ann agus porter Jerry A.
Agus bhí triplex stout on Western Star ann

Curfá (chorus) . . . too ral oo . . . etc . . .

Do bhí Seán Bán ann is a concertina,
Is ró-bhreá 'sheinn sé an Sootie Ril dóibh,
An Set of Erin is an Polka bríomhar,
An Highland Fling is an Laddie Goolie ann.

[The blessed donkeys and the cross of the saints on them,
Dawing porter without collar or harness on them,
The porter of Willie Hassett and the porter of Jerry A.
was there
And there was triplex stout from the Western Star there.

Chorus

Seán Bán was there with his concertina,
And he played the Sootie Reel very well for them,
The Set of Erin and the lively polka,
The Highland Fling and the Laddie Goolie.]

4

House Dances and Home Entertainment

Long before prosperity brought in tarpaulin and carpets, people danced with zest on the flagstone floors of homes in rural districts.

House dances with plenty of music, sets, singing, storytelling and other forms of diversion were the main source of entertainment in Sliabh Luachra until the 1920s and '30s when dance halls began to take over the social scene. Prior to the dance halls, crossroads dances had been the principal public forum for dancing.

Those attending house dances were usually invited and were generally neighbours and friends confined to a townland or two. In those days somebody in almost every house could play an instrument so there was no shortage of musicians for a set . . . good or bad. You mightn't land a lot of them up on the stage in Carnegie Hall, but they were important to the locality or side of the country for which they were always willing to play. People simply had to make their own entertainment and they did so in a homely, unpretentious way.

Money was scarce and there was no question of cash payments to musicians; neither was drink regarded as essential to enjoyment, though there might be a dozen stout in some corner of the house. Johnny O'Leary, now one of Sliabh Luachra's best-known musicians, remembers playing in his own townland of Maulykevane for up to eight hours for two bottles of stout and a cup of tea 'out of the hand'. Jig sets and polka sets were danced, the Talavara, the Jenny Lind, the Cock and the Hen and others.

The kitchen, always the largest room by far in a house, and the place where families spent most of their time, was ideal for the purpose. The better furnished parlour, where it existed, was used only occasionally and for events such as stations: the priest would have breakfast in the parlour with the man of the house and a few male neighbours. It was a no-go area otherwise.

On opening the main door of the house from outside, one was immediately in the kitchen – no hallways or conservatories then. The centrepiece of the spacious kitchen was the open fire, which seemed to burn eternally. For dancing, the table, chairs and bench seats were moved to the walls, leaving plenty of room for sets in the centre. A huge fire of turf and bog deal (bog oak) blazed in the hearth and, given that almost every house was thatched, the heat was often unbearable. Signs on, dancers shed excess avoirdupois as they stepped it out.

Such was the craze for dancing that it was easy to

fill the kitchen and sometimes there was hardly enough room for the musicians to sit down. One night at a house dance in Cordal, musicians Pádraig O'Keeffe and Paddy Cronin found themselves in such a position and the hostess asked them to step up on the table on which she placed two chairs. Drawing an analogy with the nearest chapel, Pádraig, quick-witted as ever, murmured to his companion, 'Christ, Paddy, we'll g'up in the gallery!' And they did.

If musicians were late in arriving, which they often were as they might have made some unscheduled stops in a public house along the route, a youngster might be asked to play a few tunes. If none was available, an older person might be prevailed upon to dydle for a set. Wind-up gramophones, on which 78 rpm records sent from America were played, also came in handy at times.

In those days men whistled a lot whilst working in the fields, walking the roads and at dances. Some could whistle dozens of tunes, good enough for people to dance to. An able whistler easily picked up a tune which he would practise as he went about his everyday business.

Musicians were always guaranteed a hearty welcome at house dances and were never put sitting too far away from a barrel of porter if such was available – as would be the case on special occasions. They would be handed a 'little drop' of whiskey on arrival and were kept well lubricated for the remainder of the night.

We're talking about days long before electricity illuminated the countryside. Kitchens were dimly lit by parrafin oil lamps and various other devices. Before the lamp was perfected there was only the light from the fire: they had a bog deal splinter which they lit to do work around the house or light them to bed. No talk of insurance risks, of course!

When the musicians took a break, a song was called for. Many people were quite shy about coming forward. Some were known to keep their heads down or hide behind somebody else in a corner when giving a song, especially if strangers were in the house. This despite the fact that nearly always those present were from the same district and rarely moved far outside it. It was a novelty to travel five or six miles from home for a dance. Motor cars were few and far between and people made the best of what they had in their own townlands: if they wanted to travel out they walked or went by horse and trap.

The late Paddy Coakley of Lyreatough, a traditional singer of note and a musician when the occasion demanded, used to tell of being invited to a ball night in Lisheen, Gneeveguilla, about eight miles away. He duly headed off for the house in Lisheen, carrying his melodeon in a message bag.

Paddy played for a set until some of the regular musicians turned up after the pubs closed in Gneeveguilla. A small, dark-haired fellow, also with a melodeon, then sat down beside him and started to play. Paddy, who had never heard anything quite like him, was highly impressed.

He quietly slipped his own melodeon back into the bag and moved down near the back door where he humbly spent the remainder of the night. He discovered that the young fellow was none other than John Clifford who was closely associated with the Murphy family of Lisheen (later marrying Julia Murphy) and a gifted musician.

The story illustrates the wealth of music in the area and the fact that there were many pockets within Sliabh Luachra boasting musicians who were rarely heard outside those pockets.

Not all the musicians were taught by music teachers; some picked up the music themselves by trial and error. As for dancing, children learnt on kitchen floors whilst still very young and they were not short of tutors. An old man with a stick sitting by the fire might train an expert eye on proceedings. Keeping time to the music was the real test and from the auld lad could be heard shouts of 'heel and toe' and 'square it' as they wheeled around.

Plenty of step dancers were available, many with their own individual steps and with the ability to make up steps as they went along with the music. Some indulged in gimmicks like dancing with a brush, to the delight of their audiences. Riverdance of the fireside.

When called upon, dancers would be ordered to 'get out on the flag' which was a reference to the big flagstones that were found on old mud floors. A cow's or a horse's head was sometimes buried under such stones, thus accounting for the clipped echo when touched by a dancer's feet: their idea of acoustics. The flagstones were also used for flailing corn.

Enthusiasts designed kitchens and house extensions with dancing in mind. A Knocknagree builder, the late Mick Moynihan, who was himself an avid set dancer, always made sure that any concrete floor he laid was as smooth as a sheet of glass and just right for dancing. The only problem was that if the floor got wet it could be very dangerous.

As well as house dances, each townland had a rambling house to which neighbours, men mostly, roved at night. Topics of the day were discussed, stories told and cards played. At times, there might be a few tunes, songs and dances. If there weren't enough women around to make up a polka set, eight men might get together for an all-male 'buck' set.

Rambling houses were friendly, informal places with a welcome for everyone. The door was always open; ramblers just came in, took a seat by the fire and joined in whatever was going on.

Three well-known Sliabh Luachra people – Dan O'Connell and Jimmy O'Brien, who run traditional pubs in Knocknagree and Killarney, respectively, and the actor and seanchaí Éamon Kelly – well remember the rambling houses of their youth and have given descriptions of what went on in their boyhood days.

In the words of Dan O'Connell, Sliabh Luachra was a little known place when he was growing up in the 1920s and '30s, though his native townland, Tureen, three miles from Knocknagree, was a lively spot. But people didn't move far away. For instance, Dan didn't know many people in Gneeveguilla, only six or seven miles to the west, until several years later, and was almost twenty-two years of age before he saw Killarney for the first time.

Hardly a night passed in Tureen without activity in some house. A fiddle could be found in most kitchens. Dan often saw seven or eight fiddlers playing together and recalls going from house to house to collect enough dancers for a set. Maggie Jones, Katie Healy and Katie O'Keeffe were concertina players and Hannah O'Neill, who wore the 'smallest pair of shoes ever', was one of the neatest dancers he ever saw to grace the floor. Julia Dunlea was a blind fiddler and Tadhgie Shine often drew music from a comb with paper around it.

He also recalls Peg Carroll's shop. She returned from America around 1933 and the shop she bought had a big kitchen where sets were danced almost every night. Timmy O'Keeffe used to teach the Jenny Lind and Victorian sets.

Jimmy O'Brien's local rambling house was the home of Pat and Julia Doyle, at Maulykevane (Jib), about six miles west of Gneeveguilla. Pat was a fiddler steeped in tradition. Julia was not only a sweet singer herself but also a shrewd judge of a singer. The Doyle children all played music and Jimmy is now one of Sliabh

Luachra's most popular musicians. Dan O'Leary and his nephew, Johnny O'Leary, were also visitors to the house.

O'Brien reminisces: 'We used to have tin whistles, accordeons and fiddles and you'd always be sure of a set there on Sunday evenings. We used to make an awful lot of noise and Julia would say, 'Will ye shut up, my head is in a bodhrán.' That was the first time I heard of a bodhrán. She'd try to stop us, but she didn't want to stop us really. They were marvellous people. "The Blind Beggar" was one of Julia's favourite songs.'

He also has happy memories of great nights in houses like Andy Thade McCarthy's, in his own townland of Lyreatough.

There were regular callers to Éamon Kelly's home at Carrigeen, roughly half-way between Barraduff and Killarney. From the men who visited he picked up some of the inspiration that made him Ireland's supreme storyteller.

Music in our townland was the concertina played by a Mrs Moynihan (Katie Dan) and also by Brian and Michael Kelly. They played at the house dances, as did fiddlers like John Cronin, of Cornhill, and the Fitzgerald brothers, of Artigallivan. Members of the Williams family, Brewsterfield, were great musicians – Henry (fiddle), Michael (accordeon) and Barry, their father, on pipes. The old man was a spirited step dancer and, at the age of eighty, danced on the runway at Shannon Airport when seeing some people off to America. The Williamses were regular visitors to house dances when I was young. There was often a break for a story, not of the formal, traditional kind, but more of an elongated anecdote.[1]

As well as house dances, several other events with dancing as a central feature took place in the homes of Sliabh Luachra fifty or sixty years ago. Nearly all have disappeared, but the stations is a survivor that still thrives. One house in each station district of the parish was chosen to host the stations on a rota basis. The stations began with Mass being celebrated in the house, always a memorable occasion for family, relations and neighbours. In recent times, some clergy have discouraged the post-Mass festivities, especially excessive drinking, but a party nearly always takes place when the religious ceremonies of the day are over and sets are danced well into the next day.

Long ago when folk were not as house-proud as they are now, frenzied preparations preceded stations. Houses were cleaned and painted, walls whitewashed, yards brushed and heaps of manure removed from sight. The arrival of the priest generated some apprehension. In times gone by, half-tierces of stout would be hidden from his view and covered with a coarse bag.

Only work that was absolutely necessary would be done that day. Men and women wore their best clothes all day. Plenty of food and drink would be available for everybody. The night was given over to jollification, much like a house dance but with a more profound sense of occasion.

Wedding receptions (then called breakfasts) were also held in houses. The wedding party would go to the church in a sidecar or horse and trap for the nuptials. Afterwards, there was no question of going to a hotel. It was back to the house where generous helpings of food and drink were laid out for the guests. Following some speeches, the entertainment would begin with polka sets, step dances from children and a few songs.

People who didn't attend at the chapel in the morning would come at night for more celebrations. Strawboys, who hadn't been invited, would also invariably arrive at the wedding house that night. They would be covered in straw and well disguised in colourful costumes. The captain of the group would ask if there was any objection to strawboys. They were almost always made welcome and then walked in, dancing with whoever was available. They would each be given a mug of porter and would leave after a set. Strawboys brought vivacity and excitement to the scene and gave youngsters a wonderful thrill. The practice lives on in a few areas, especially in the County Cork side of Sliabh Luachra, notably around Cullen.

'Eating the Gander' was another occasion for music and dance. It came after a match being made between a prospective bride and groom and was held in the bride's house when the 'bindings' (legal arrangements) were made and the way cleared for marriage.

The 'biddy ball' was regarded as one of the most enjoyable social events of the year. A group would get together, disguise themselves and dress up in strange clothes. Accompanied by musicians and dancers they would go from house to house over a wide area on the night of 31 January–1 February (feast of St Brigid), collecting money as they went. The custom was known as 'going out in the biddy'. Some weeks later a biddy ball would be organised in a house with a large kitchen. Proceeds would go towards the purchase of porter, food and other refreshments. Shop bread, when available, would be on the menu, and it was a rarity at the time as country people baked all their own bread, cakes as big as car wheels with spokes cut across them. Well plastered with red jam, shop bread was nouvelle cuisine.

Unlike the house dances, people from outside the immediate area would be invited to the biddy ball, and they were sometimes asked to make a small contribution to the cost of the ball. Music and dancing would go on all night and the sun would usually be high in the sky when revellers went home next day.

The biddy tradition has undergone something of a revival in recent times, but a significant difference is that money raised is given to charity.

An event which involved far less organisation was the threshing dance which took place at harvest time when oats and other grain were being threshed (pronounced 'thrashed') in farmyards. The coming of the thresher with its distinct whine echoeing through the countryside was an occasion to be savoured – an event with its own unique magic.

A *meitheal* (group of people helping each other) would gather to assist in the operation and when the work was done a dance was held in the farmhouse with a few bottles of stout opened to restore lost energy. Paddy Doyle of Jib had a thresher in the 1950s and he always took his melodeon around with him. The threshing marked the end of the working year for the farming community. With all crops safely in, it was a landmark date and a time to celebrate a fruitful harvest.

Ball nights were often held in rural houses. A group of people would agree to contribute so much towards the cost of a few drinks and would gather at a certain house for a dance. Girls were invited free of charge in most places.

An American wake was a social occasion always tinged with sadness. It was a get-together on the eve of the departure to America of a person from a locality. The young man or woman about to leave would be the star of the night, during which sets would be danced and porter quaffed. There would be songs about emigration, such as 'The Shores of Amerikay' and 'The Home I left Behind', sometimes rendered by the exile-to-be, adding further poignancy to the gathering.

As many of those going away never again returned, there was an air of finality and a feeling of seeing someone for the last time, but some prankster always lightened proceedings with a funny song or practical joke.

In some areas, neighbours would accompany the new exile to the nearest railway station on the following day. Last farewells would be exchanged with family and friends and there would be heart-rending scenes on the station platform as the train steamed out on its lonely journey to meet a waiting ocean liner in Queenstown (now Cobh), County Cork.

5

Dance halls and Changing Trends

From the mid-1920s a new phenomenon began to dominate the entertainment scene. Dance halls mushroomed all over the place, often within a few a miles of one another, and dances in halls gradually took over from house dances.

Enterprising individuals, some of whom were already in other businesses, built the halls which, generally speaking, were cheaply-constructed, corrugated-iron structures with wooden frames, at crossroads and villages all over Sliabh Luachra. Most were without running water and other basic facilities, but once the owner had provided a stage, a timber floor and a roof, he was up and away. Drink was off limits, but at least one of the halls had a shebeen which was noted for the quality of its poteen – an added attraction.

Musicians abounded and they now found a bigger platform for their talents. Another change was that they were also paid a few shillings for their work. Plenty of dancers were available, but they had a problem – a shortage of money. The admission fee to a hall might be only a few pence in old money, but that was hard to come by in bad times. Due to factors like the Economic War with Britain, farmers were short of cash. Farmers usually had big families and many boys and girls on farms got very little pay for their work. Neither was any off-farm employment available and emigration was very high.

A factor militating against dance halls was clerical opposition. In the context of what happens nowadays, it's hard to understand the zeal with which clergy tried to close down halls. They had also been known to break up house dances.

In the parish of Rathmore, a curate, Fr O'Connor, achieved notoriety for the vehemence of his anti-dancing campaign. As meeting places for the sexes, halls were seen as 'occasions of sin' and hall-owners were sometimes condemned from the altar. In a few extreme cases, priests refused to accept dues, oats money and other payments from them. However, many halls survived and prospered.

Dances were held on Sunday evenings and in a bid to stop dancing in Thady Willie O'Connor's hall in Gneeveguilla, Fr O'Connor started a holy hour in the local chapel at the same time. The dancing continued.[1]

One of the first halls in Sliabh Luachra was Vaughan's in Ballydesmond, opened in 1924. Several others sprung up in the second half of the twenties and they came into their own in the thirties, forties and fifties. Halls speckled the landscape and dancers had ample choice.

Thady Willie O'Connor's hall opened in Gneeveguilla in 1927 and was among the best venues. In spite of having a sheet-iron roof, wonderful sound could be generated in the hall. A small farmer, Thady was a dapper, smartly-spoken man with a flair for business; an impresario of his time. He charged 2p admission and personally welcomed each patron with a warm handshake. Smiling Thady was also known to go on stage and ask the 'boys' (some might be forty years and over) to dance with the 'strange' girls. A girl didn't have to come from too far away to be a stranger. She might have arrived by bike from, say Boherbue, eight or nine miles distant, but, as people didn't move too far, few would know her.

Apart from Thady's natural courtesy there was a very practical reason for ensuring that all girls got a dance: if they didn't they might never again be seen in his hall.

The cream of Sliabh Luachra musicians played in the hall – the Murphys of Lisheen, Pádraig O'Keeffe, the Cronins, John Clifford, Johnny O'Leary and numerous others, and dances were held there right through the showband era up to the early eighties. Thady, who died in 1974 at the age of 88, was one of the great characters of the area. His son, Jim, was also a lively character known only as Jim Thady Willie. Jim ran the hall for many years and he died in May 1999.

A huge volume of folklore has survived from the era of the humble country hall. By all accounts, as much fun was had going to and coming from the hall as actually happened during dances. 'Transport being nonexistent, people walked to halls in groups. The exception, the proud owner of a bicycle, was more to be pitied than envied as that person spent more time carrying the bicycle than it was carrying him, owing to the poor state of roads and inferior tyres. Neither was the bicycle designed to carry two extra passengers who booked seats on the crossbar and carrier. There was many a mishap.'[2]

Ruses had also to be devised to a put a few pence together to get into a dance. A chicken, a dozen eggs or a sack of potatoes might be stolen from the farm and sold to raise cash.

Practical jokes were played on the way home in the darkness, with pebbles being thrown at windows, strings tied to door latches and gates taken from pillars. The odd donkey was also taken on temporary loan to get a tired dancer home.

Many of the gas-lit halls survived the so-called Emergency during World War II (1939-45) and the late forties heralded a more liberal era. You could dance in Gneeveguilla in the afternoon and then head for Ballydesmond, six miles away, where another dance began at 7.00 pm.

Some hall-owners laid on transport for patrons. Peter Murphy of Lacca, just on the County Cork side of the Blackwater, used his lorry to bring crowds to his popular hall. His musicians included Pádraig O'Keeffe. One night, Pádraig, who had a few pints taken, was late getting on board and his usual seat in front of the lorry had been taken by someone else. He then had to jump into the back with the rest of the crowd. As the lorry rounded a few sharp bends on the road between Scartaglen and Ballydesmond the hilarious Pádraig rolled to one side with the crowd and was heard to shout at the driver, 'Slow down, or I'll spill!'

Peter Murphy, a returned Yank, would, according to those who knew him, go anywhere for music. His hall was one of the nicest ever seen.[3] The inside walls were skirted by brightly-painted ceiling boards, seats were placed all around the sides and the building was kept in a tidy state. Peter also had the best of musicians on the bandstand, such as Pádraig O'Keeffe, the Murphys of Lisheen, and Jack and Denny O'Sullivan of Ballydaly.

But Peter had an eventful twelve years as a dance hall proprietor and had survived several brushes with the clergy. Petrol shortages following the outbreak of World War II put an end to Peter's transport service and led to a sharp drop in business. His hall closed around 1940.

In the early years of the dance halls, jig sets and polka sets dominated the repertoire, but things gradually changed. Accordeonist Johnny O'Leary, who began his playing career in Toremore hall in 1934 at the age of twelve, says that in halls like Thady Willie's they initially played three sets and three old-time waltzes during a dance. In time, that was reduced to two sets and two waltzes to allow for more modern dances which began to creep in during the forties.

Eventually, foxtrots and tangoes as well as the twist, rock 'n' roll and pop music all but swept traditional dances aside in the 1950s. Radio was also a critical influence, with trendy stations such as Radio Luxembourg enjoying a massive listenership amongst young people.

The forties were good times for the halls and many had annual 'big nights'. In Ballydesmond it was the teachers' dance while Scartaglen was a red-letter date on St Stephen's Night. People always dressed in their best clothes when going to the hall. Men wore suits and the fair sex turned out in chic skirts and cardigans. Liberal lacings of Brylcreem kept a fellow's hair in place and bicycle clips were put into the jacket pocket during the dance.

Romance frequently blossomed. Courtship was conducted on the way home and haysheds were a warm, safe haven for lovers, even if the odd one was set on fire by cigarette butts.

After the war, people moved about more easily. Bicycle tyres could be obtained once more and petrol was available for the few people with cars. Most patrons didn't drink and a whiff of alcohol was almost certain to result in a girl refusing a dance request. If a fellow was drunk at a dance, they'd be talking about him for a week after. A man had also to be a reasonably good dancer to ensure that he got a partner on the floor. Certain individuals couldn't put a step together and as they were quickly noted women became adept at dodging their advances.

Late night and extension dances which went on well after midnight were introduced, giving rise to new customs. Supper became a feature, with houses close to halls opening their parlours to provide food for dancers. You could have a plain tea, consisting of tea, bread and butter and jam, or if you were really serious about a girl you'd make a 'dacent' man of yourself by treating her to a 'meat tea' which included a hearty plate of shop ham.

Some entrepreneurs opened bike parking facilities close to halls. They used spare rooms or their backyards where 'high nellies' could be safely deposited for a modest fee until the night was over.

Other houses close to halls served as make-up rooms for girls on their way to a dance. In such houses girls would give themselves a final touch-up whilst having a cup of tea. They would change into their best shoes, which they would have brought with them in a bag, backcomb the hair, puff powder their faces, rub on a little rouge to highlight their cheekbones and finish off the beautification process with a compulsory coating of red lipstick.

What glamour!

Cars, Ballrooms and Bigger Bands

The growing popularity of the motorcar in post-war years was one of the factors that brought about the end of small halls. Also from the mid-forties onwards bigger bands began to replace local musicians: many of the smaller halls closed and were converted into stores and garages, deserted by dancers who travelled to neighbouring towns which had modern bands and bigger, swankier halls – generally given the posh title of ballroom.

Some traditional musicians formed céilí bands and among the best known in Sliabh Luachra was the Desmond, which featured different musicians from time to time. A regular in the band was Michael O'Callaghan who lives in Castleisland. Musicians like Denis Murphy, Johnny O'Leary, Mikey Duggan, Jimmy Doyle, Neilus O'Connor, Jack O'Regan, Tom Fitzgerald, Denis McMahon, Donal and Patrick O'Connor, Aeneas O'Connell, Marian Fitzmaurice, Tom Fleming, Frank Dennison, Nicky and Anne McAuliffe, members of the O'Callaghan family and others featured at various times.

The Brosna Céilí Band was also very much in demand while colourful Scartaglen personality John 'Tailor' Brosnan formed the O'Rahilly Céilí Band in the late forties. The line-up included people like Willie Reidy, Jerry McCarthy, Timmy Spillane, Dan Cronin, Mary McQuinn (vocals) and the Tailor himself on drums. With new trends in the fifties when dancers looked for more modern music, Brosnan's band evolved into the Radiant Showband and new members, some with saxophones, replaced most of the traditional musicians.

Times were changing rapidly and Irish dancing was taking a back seat. Some of the best traditional musicians in the area, such as Denis Murphy and the

Cronin brothers, to mention just a handful, were forced to emigrate in the late forties and fifties and their departure was a serious loss to the music and the dance halls. Like hundreds of other musicians they took the boat to America where, ironically, traditional music enjoyed a boom in the fifties and sixties.

At home, people began to look abroad for entertainment. Very little time was given to traditional music on radio while rock and pop music were broadcast on a daily basis. Traditional music was not the 'in thing' and it suffered greatly. It was seen as being old fashioned and belonging to a poorer era with a pronounced rural image which people disowned at the time. They were not keen to learn Irish music or dancing and a generation would pass before 'trad' became fashionable again.

Some enthusiasts argue that the music was in grave danger of extinction in the fifties and early sixties and might have disappeared altogether but for a hard core of truly loyal people who kept it going in the area against the tide.[4] The establishment of Comhaltas Ceoltóirí Éireann (CCÉ) in 1951 gave a much-needed impetus to the music nationally and the organisation later became active in Sliabh Luachra.

Many of the céilí bands, including the Desmond, had to have modern music in their repertoire to meet public demand. Nicky McAuliffe, who now gives traditional music classes in Sliabh Luachra, first played with the Desmond in Gneeveguilla hall on St Patrick's Night 1964. While basically a céilí band, he says they had to play a mixture of everything to satisfy demands. The Desmond competed in All-Ireland Fleadhanna Cheoil and finished second in the Oireachtas in 1968 and '69.

Several radio broadcasts were made by the Desmond, one of the best being with the late Seán Ó Murchú on the *Céilí House* programme at the RTÉ studios, Cork, in 1969. The band also appeared on television.

The economic boom of the sixties and the glamour of the showband era killed off most of the small rural dance halls, with Vaughan's and Jim Thady Willie's (both of which still stand) being among the last to close in the early eighties. By and large, young Sliabh Luachra people were now in reasonably-paid jobs, mainly in factories that had opened in towns surrounding the area, such as Killarney. More people could also afford their own cars and it was much easier, as a result, to travel to huge ballrooms like the Gleneagle, in Killarney, and the Hi-land, Newmarket, which drew thousands of dancers from a wide area . . . a world removed from the simple, intimate country halls where their parents had met not all that many years before.

6

Storytelling and Yarnspinning

Shadows of leaping flames dance on the whitewashed kitchen walls and everyone is gathered round the hearth. Expectation fills the air. Only one man speaks; all the others sit silently, giving him their complete attention as he weaves his own spell with words that echo through generations past.

Another night of storytelling is underway and the only light is that thrown out by the blazing turf fire. This is theatre of the fireside. The rapt audience waits and listens, eager to be enthralled.

Before the written word, the seanchaí was the book, library and newspaper of his local community. He was also the local historian and an authority on the lore of the district; a genealogist who could trace relationships, someone who knew the countryside, the names of fields, landmarks and the stories behind the names.

Much of the history, folklore and tradition of Sliabh Luachra has been passed on through word of mouth. The people have always been known as great talkers with colourful turns of phrase and a rich oral heritage.

In days long ago, some who were illiterate as far as the printed word was concerned could reel off long and detailed accounts of historic events and famous personalities: and they could also recite poetry at length, having learnt all the verses by heart.

Remember, even in the last century, not everyone could read and write, so that the only way people kept themselves informed of what was happening in their localities and in the wider world was by oral means. The ability to relate and embellish a good yarn was, and still is, regarded as a gift in itself, with wit and a punchline being essential to the enjoyment of listeners. One of the best practitioners of the art in the area today is Jim Barry of Tureendarby.

Storytelling seems to have formed a large part of the entertainment of rambling houses in the countryside. In *Leabhar Sheáin Ui Chonaill* (written by the famous South Kerry storyteller), we're told how in Cill Rialaigh, near Ballinskelligs, people went at night to a house in the village where the best storyteller was to be found.

Stories were based on happenings in the district, but mostly in the old days they related to the Fianna and were handed down from father to son. Local characters like the Black Rogue of Glenflesk featured in stories. Men of the roads (not travellers in the modern sense) were good storytellers and brought news of the world outside. Such men were welcome in rambling houses in wintertime and there was a tradition in some places of keeping a bed by the fire called *leabaidh na mbocht* (the poor man's bed).

Nearly always, storytellers were men, but the most famous seanchaí of our own time, Éamon Kelly, knew a woman storyteller from Valentia, whilst his mother, Hannah, used to tell of the ghost of Béalnadeaga.

The Kelly home at Carrigeen was a rambling house.[1] The Kellys themselves, though known for their wit and way with words, were not storytellers in the traditional sense but, according to Éamon, some men visiting the house could 'put a good face to a story' when the occasion demanded. Every adventure of the day at a fair, market, wake, wedding, or working in the fields was told as a story. It was always men who went rambling at night (women did their visitation during the day) and some had stories to tell about Eoghan Rua Ó Súilleabháin, Daniel O'Connell, or Dean Swift. These stories came up in general conversation and the tellers didn't settle themselves to tell as would the traditional storytellers who had died out in Éamon's district before he was born.

Éamon Kelly's first time seeing a traditional storyteller was when he went to Waterville as a young vocational teacher and met Irish-speaking storytellers from Ballinskelligs. Prior to that, however, he had been touched by the oral tradition of Sliabh Luachra as he went to work at an early age with his father, Ned, who was a carpenter and builder.

The work brought him into the homes of the people

and he also met journeymen and stonemasons who were very interesting characters with stories to relate. He remembers such people as being fairly literate and very much steeped in what he describes as oral literature. He unconsciously picked up stories from them, stories that were as old as time itself. One man might specialise in fairy stories, while a favourite topic was experiences they had at night, seeing things, and other hair-raising yarns. They had a great facility for talk and speech in those days.

While teaching in Listowel, Éamon met the late Bryan MacMahon, became interested in drama and took parts in plays. He joined the Radio Éireann Players from the amateur drama scene as did his wife, Maura O'Sullivan, who comes from Listowel.[2]

But he became a storyteller by accident. At a Radio Éireann party he told a story he had heard in south Kerry. Micheál Ó hAodha, then head of entertainment programmes, was impressed and asked him to go on a programme as a result. When Éamon went around the country afterwards people who had heard him on radio gave him stories. 'By throwing my mind back to my young days and remembering small fragments I made them into the stories I told,' he explains.

The stories were something quite new on radio and appealed to a very large audience. I remember as a young boy growing up in Gneeveguilla being left stay up late on Saturday nights just to hear the seanchaí on programmes like *The Rambling House*. Some of the characters in Éamon's stories were identifiable locally and provided ample food for conversation as people left the chapel after Mass the following morning. Phrases from his stories, like 'in my father's time' and 'things rested so', became popular cants at the time.

Kelly succeeded in bringing the craft of the storyteller to the stage. His one-man shows, such as *Bless Me Father* and *According to Custom*, were notable successes. With an actor's acute sense of timing and feel for an audience, he moved effortlessly from one story to the next, helped by his inflection and gestures. The stage settings re-created the kitchen of a Kerry cottage of the 1920s with rafters, an open hearth with hobs and a soot-black crane for the kettle and pots. Socks hung over the fire to dry and household appurtenances were placed here and there – just like the homes Éamon Kelly was familiar with as a child.

Sitting in a theatre, one was taken back in time and Kelly looked the part of a seanchaí with his hat being the most critical part of his dress. His shirt had a stud closing the top, but no collar or tie. There was the essential waistcoat over which he wore a short coat. He used the hat as a prop to tell the stories. His father always wore a hat, he says, and never took it off except to go to bed, or to the church and 'as my mother would say he slept in both.'

7

A Blind Fiddler and his Donkey

The blind fiddler and music teacher, Tom Billy Murphy (1875–1943), was one of the unforgettable characters of Sliabh Luachra, whose physical disablities only added to his mystique. The sharpness of his other faculties compensated in some way for his blindness for he could, in the lyrical words of Johnny O'Leary, hear a honeybee walking.

He was a man who saw music not only in the countless notes he played, but also in words. Though not blessed with a good singing voice, he was renowned, for instance, for the way he would take a standard ballad and recite it in the manner another person would a poem.

He is still remembered as a man who all his life travelled the scattered area on a saddled donkey, with the faithful animal following the route from house to house along a complicated network of bohereens. They used to say that Tom could identify a house from the distinctive smell of the smoke that rose from its chimney.

Tom had a remarkable rapport with his donkey, which he looked on as an intelligent, understanding animal. Whoever spread the rumour that donkeys are stupid animals was well wide of the mark and did a grave injustice to an animal that has been badly treated in many ways. Donkeys are quite smart and have been known to go to the creamery and home again, or bring loads of turf from the bog, without the guidance of man. Tom and others realised that well.

It was said that Tom Billy knew a bohereen leading to an intended destination by the sound of his donkey's hooves. He and his guide donkey were inseparable and their journeys have inspired poets and others. In the poem 'Twinned Vision' by Tadhg Ua Duinnín, the donkey gives an insight into their travels:

I guided you
all your ways
in the bright
and the dark days;
they were all just dark to you
– dark as night –
and somehow,
secretly,
instinctively
I knew . . .
I knew you were blind;
I had to find your way.

Tom Billy was born in Glencollins, Ballydesmond, County Cork, in February 1875, and was one of seventeen children in the family of William (Billy) and Catherine Murphy (née Herlihy). The Murphys were comfortable farmers by local standards and had lived in the area for generations. Even though Tom was to become an outstanding cultural figure, life was not easy for him in his youth. His mother died when he was only eight years of age. At thirteen, he became partly paralysed as a result of suspected polio. He lost his sight and was left with limited use of one leg and one hand.

Regarded as a bright pupil, he attended the local national school until he was fifteen, and is said to have been particularly good at Irish and English, with a facility to quote from Shakespeare when such quotations were applicable to local events. His musical talent was also noted and he took up the fiddle as a hobby. By the time he left school he was well able to play and music became his livelihood. His talent was nurtured by a roving music teacher, Tadhg Buckley (Taidhgín an Asail), from nearby Knocknagree, who went around the locality on a donkey and regularly visited Tom's home.

There are many stories about Tom Billy, who was clearly a many-sided, clever man with a natural capacity for gaeity and friendship. A nephew, Brother Hilary Murphy, who now lives in the Presentation Monastery, Killarney, says he was taken absolutely for granted as if he were part of the landscape 'sitting on his donkey going by, turning his coat collar up as the first thin blowing of rain met him, or silhouetted against the sky going up the steep Knocknaboul road on his way to Tír na nÓg as he used to call the land of mystery to the west – County Kerry'.

Another memory is of people in a meadow saving hay suddenly hearing the distant sound of a tin whistle drawing ever closer . . . as Tom and his donkey slowly approach along the road, all work ceases and the enthralled haymakers just stand and listen.

According to his grandniece, Catherine Murphy, who has collected family memories of the musician, he was anything but remote, even if he looked to be in a world of his own. 'He had great compassion and an enormous capacity for sympathy . . . He could certainly communicate with the young and could easily distinguish different voices and was never mistaken even in the sound of footsteps.'[1]

Anybody who ever knew Tom Billy was struck by his gift of being able to gladden hearts; he was a man who made light of his disabilities and developed his talents for his own satisfaction and the enjoyment of others. Though he never married himself he had the confidence of young lovers who were known to seek his wise counsel.

Tom Billy was regarded as a straightforward fiddler who didn't go in much for ornamentation and used the ABC method, dictating the notes which his pupils wrote down. He taught music in homes on both sides of the Cork–Kerry border, specialising in fiddle and tin whistle. He might stay in a house for a week, or more, teaching during the day and entertaining the growns-ups and their neighbours at night. That was the way he lived, continually moving from house to house and staying in each for a while before resuming his musical circuit.

He acquired a broad repertoire and had well over a hundred reels, but, like many another musician, took a deal of his tunes to the grave. One of his pupils, Molly Myers Murphy, has the biggest collection of his tunes, many of which have been published by the late Breandán Breathnach, and are now in the Traditional Music Archive, 63 Merrion Square, Dublin.[2] Her hundreds of tunes, meticulously written out by herself in copy-books, are, in the words of Mr Breathnach, 'the greatest contribution to a collection of Irish music made by any lady musician'.

Molly was only ten years old when she had her first lesson on the fiddle from Tom at her home near Farranfore, County Kerry, in 1926.

> Tom's arrival was always a big occasion and he once stayed with us for about three months, including Christmas. He'd give you a few tunes to learn and would come back several months later to see how how you were getting on. When Tom was around there was plenty of fun and he had an awful lot of poems off by heart. I remember well how he kept us up all night on one occasion

> reciting 113 verses. He had an amazing sense of presence and would know people by their footsteps. He always knew when people were in a room, even if they held their breath and didn't make a sound. If he only met you once, he'd know you by your voice again.

Molly married Tom's nephew, Willie Murphy, and the couple live at Valleymount House, Glencollins, Ballydesmond.

Dressed in a typical countryman's peak cap, dark coat, baggy trousers and strong boots, Tom was a familiar figure at fairs, races, feiseanna, house parties, weddings and at public gatherings of every description along the Cork–Kerry border. A man with a liking for black porter and good company, he also played in pubs and was welcome wherever he went. 'His slip jigs and reels were shot through with abandon and conspicuous gaeity. He played his hornpipes in a smooth, long, lazy rhythm that, perhaps, did not please everybody.'[3]

Johnny O'Leary's late uncle Dan was one of his pupils, and Johnny still has graphic recollections of Tom, whom he remembers as having very big ears, coming to their home.

> Tom was grand once you took down music right and played it as it should be played, but he'd go mad if you didn't do it the way he wanted it done. He was a hard teacher, but a very good one. He'd

> play all day. Very little money changed hands as most people had nothing. He might get a few bottles of stout and after three or four days there'd be a collection for a dance in some house for him. He'd be lucky to go away with thirteen or fourteen shillings.

While staying in a house, Tom would share in whatever was going and bunk in with the others. 'I slept in the same bed with him. He'd one very cold leg and if it touched you at all you'd go through the ceiling. But he was mighty craic – fierce witty,' said Johnny with a laugh.

Like several other musicians in the area, Tom appears to have been at his best when playing slow airs, of which he had many. These he preferred to play for chosen listeners who appreciated the songs related to the airs, such as 'Bean Dubh an Ghleanna', 'An Raibh Tú ar an gCarraig?' and 'Caoine an Spailpín'.

Before playing such airs, Tom was in the habit of telling the stories behind them, giving insights into past events in either national or local history. He had several poems and ballads memorised and loved to recite them with passion and deep feeling. Again, he would preface a rendering with the historical background so that his audience would know exactly what it was all about.

Unfortunately, there are no known recordings of his music as he died a few years before the necessary technology became common. But the romantic image of

Tom Billy and his donkey will linger on and he will be remembered for passing on the music of Sliabh Luachra through his pupils. His tunes, some known simply as Tom Billy's, are still played.

He has also been immortalised in Tadhg Ua Duinnín's perceptive verses, which reflect his lifestyle as the poet sees it through the eyes of the donkey:

My eyes were
your windows
open wide
to the road
and skies
and yet,
you scanned a wider field
than the heartland of Sliabh Luachra
thro' the magic lantern
of your mind
behind those shuttered eyes.

Tom suffered a stroke whilst staying in Molly Myers Murphy's old home on a warm, sunny day in July 1943. He died on 1 November that year, in Nazareth Home, Mallow, having spent well over forty years as a true wandering minstrel, and was buried in Ballydesmond cemetery.

Another well-known musician in Ballydesmond in Tom Billy's time was Din Tarrant, a carpenter whose work took him around a wide area. As well as being a fine fiddler with polkas as a specialty, he was reputed to have been an exceptional craftsman. Din Tarrant's nephew, Denis Doody, is a prominent Sliabh Luachra musician today. Din, who is believed to have got much of his music from Taidhgín an Asail, was not a music teacher, but he was very much in demand for house dances and other occasions. He often played with Pádraig O'Keeffe and Tom Billy.

8

Pádraig O'Keeffe

LAST OF THE FIDDLE MASTERS

The belief in some quarters that real artists often find greater glory in death is certainly true of Pádraig O'Keeffe, who died in 1963. He has posthumously earned a level of fame that he could never have dreamed of in his heyday as a musician. His professional career would have been close to the bottom of the points table in today's terms.

His talents notwithstanding, he was a poor man, often despised by the respectability. He lost his job as a primary school teacher quite early in life; was a social outcast in the eyes of some; a man who spent many of his days and nights in pubs and someone who generally led a bohemian existence.

Unfortunately for Pádraig (he was locally known as Patrick Keeffe), he lived at a time when traditional music was not in vogue and he was scarcely known outside his native County Kerry. He missed out on the television era and also to a large extent on radio, which recorded his music when he was past his best. Ironically, however, it has been largely through radio that the music of O'Keeffe and of his many distinguished pupils has come to be recognised and appreciated. He has passed on a huge legacy in the form of hundreds of very old tunes, neatly written out by himself for pupils on now yellowing pages of copybooks and even on the back of cigarette packets. He is the most renowned of the many music teachers in the area and he also had more pupils than anybody else.

Whilst undoubtedly a superb fiddle player, his greatest achievement has been the manner in which he handed on the music. This gives him the leading position in the pantheon of Sliabh Luachra musicians and also a major place on the national scene. O'Keeffe is an outstanding figure in an era when traditional music is enjoying popularity that he could never have envisaged. There is a tendency amongst some musicians to hold back tunes from one another, but those who knew the fiddle master are adamant that that could not be said of him.

A bronze bust of O'Keeffe, which proudly dominates the village green in Scartaglen, a place in which he spent much of his time playing music, is evidence that the wheel has come full circle for a sad and tragic figure in many respects. He is now amongst the immortals of music.

Any available photographs depict an ageing, world-weary and wrinkled face that had seen a hard life, but the facial features on the memorial are of a younger, sharper man. His cap is tilted sideways towards his right ear and he gazes westward over rolling farmland towards Killarney. The bow is held in his right hand and the fiddle stands erect pointing towards his left shoulder. Beneath, an inscription in Irish and in English says simply, 'Last of the fiddle masters of Sliabh Luachra.'

Pádraig O'Keeffe was born in Glounthane – a highland district between Ballydesmond and Castleisland, in 1887 – the eldest of nine children. His father, John O'Keeffe, was principal teacher in the nearby primary school and a man with a stern reputation; his mother was Margaret O'Callaghan, who hailed from Doon, Kiskeam, over the border in County Cork. It was from his mother's side of the family that he brought the music and he once claimed to be able to tune a fiddle when he was only four years of age. The O'Callaghans were a well known musical and dancing family and Margaret's brother, Cal, was a very good fiddle player who had a strong influence on Pádraig. The O'Callaghans got much of their music from Corney Drew, a blind fiddler in their area, and unusual tunes which Pádraig played in later life came from Drew, who had inherited music from the late 18th and early 19th centuries.

Pádraig spent a lot of his youth in Doon, where he learnt a great deal of music. At the prompting of his parents, he reluctantly went on to train as a primary teacher in Dublin, and took up a number of temporary posts in Kerry before succeeding his father as principal teacher in Glounthane, in May 1915, where he was to remain until his dismissal from the job five years later.

Some of his pupils have described him as a first-class teacher[1], but the discipline of having to teach them every day and spend his time within the walls of a school was too much for his free, artistic spirit to bear. He was in trouble with the Department of Education for not turning up in school regularly, for not keeping records and for showing a lack of enthusiasm for the job. It is said that he was rarely, if ever, in school on the day after receiving his salary cheque, which would be spent on a drinking spree. He kept a fiddle hanging on the wall in school and would play at lunchtime.

After getting at least five chances from the school authorities he was eventually replaced by another teacher, in 1920. That was the end of his life in the classroom and he devoted his remaining forty-three years to teaching and playing music – his true vocation. His audiences were small and they could be found in country pubs or remote farmhouses where a boy or girl with an ear for music eagerly awaited the arrival of the master.

In his hands a fiddle became an instrument of enchantment. He could keep audiences spellbound for instance with his playing of 'The Old Man Rocking the Cradle' in which he made the fiddle intone 'mama, mama'. For this novel tune which is based on a lullaby, he would put a large door key in his mouth and use it to mute the fiddle: the 'mama' sound, like that of a baby crying, would result.

Pádraig never owned a car. He cycled occasionally but he nearly always travelled on foot, walking the roads of Sliabh Luachra with a distinctive stride, frequently covering twenty or twenty-five miles a day in all kinds of weather. He stood at around six feet in height and was a strongly-built man with a fine mop of curling hair under a tightly-fitting peaked cap. He smoked Woodbine cigarettes.

He is remembered from his younger days as being well-spoken, clean, tidy and having a pleasant manner. He was very gentle and kind in his approach and people would remark on his unusual, fast walking style.[2]

According to one of his most accomplished surviving pupils, Paddy Cronin, O'Keeffe was the best music teacher of his generation and he gave endless time to pupils in his efforts to ensure that they got the tunes right. When it came to imparting music, he was never in a hurry, even though a visit to a pub might be the next thing on his mind. An emphatic instruction to play slowly is something that has remained firmly etched on Paddy's mind.

Pádraig had an easily understood, ingenious system of writing music, with the figures 0, 1, 2, 3, 4 denoting the fingers of the left hand. The spaces between the five lines were used to show where the four strings of the fiddle were. This system, which he may have devised himself, was also used for teaching other instruments. He charged sixpence (2.5p) per tune and it is estimated that he handed on up to a thousand tunes in this manner though former pupils such as Johnny O'Leary believe that he took at least as many more tunes to the grave.

Some pupils went to great lengths to receive lessons from Pádraig and there is one story of a pupil from the Taur area who used to ride a chainless bike all the way to Glounthane: given the uphill, downhill nature of the road, it was a practice that made perfect sense.

In order to meet popular local demand from dancers, Pádraig played plenty of slides and polkas, but his preference was for reels and his specialty – slow airs. Although he was known for the sweetness of his playing, there was a haunting, lonesome quality to his airs – some of which are in the RTÉ archives. They can also be heard on a very worthwhile cassette produced by Peter Browne, of RTÉ radio.[3] His style of playing airs such as 'O'Rahilly's Grave' (most likely a lament for the poet Aodhagán Ó Rathaille) reflected the hardship of his own life.

Peter Browne says that the recordings on the tape are the best available of O'Keeffe and even if they come from the later part of his life there's reason to be grateful that the light of his rare genius shines through from an earlier and outstanding period in traditional music.

West Limerick musician Dónal de Barra believes that the ups and downs of O'Keeffe's life influenced his music and made it all the better. 'People sometimes ask what is the difference between the music of O'Keeffe and that of other musicians. I think it's like the difference between prose and poetry. In O'Keeffe's music there was poetry,' maintains de Barra, a former president of CCÉ.

Pádraig remained single and he used to call the fiddle 'the missus', declaring that it gave no bit of trouble at all. 'Just one stroke across the belly and she purrs,' he would say. In his younger days, he had a long-running romance with a neighbouring girl, Abbie Scollard, who, despite his heavy drinking, remained loyal to him and did her best to persuade him to keep his drinking to moderate levels. When the subject of marriage was raised with the O'Keeffes by a member of Abbie's family, the question was apparently ruled out by Pádraig's mother, who felt he shouldn't marry below his station. In any case Abbie emigrated to America, where she later married and had a family.

Pádraig was a private man who didn't discuss deeply intimate matters such as his broken relationship and the loss of his teaching job, but there are people who believe that Abbie Scollard's departure from Glounthane affected him traumatically, even if he didn't let on in public. However, he never indicated any regrets about having to leave Glounthane school, except perhaps with regard to the financial loss.

Throughout his life he had very little money, but always liked to have the price of a pint of stout in his pocket as he faced into a pub. He looked on that as a 'seed' and once he had money for the first one his listeners and friends would keep him supplied with pints and halves of whiskey for the remainder of an evening.

Always cracking jokes, he loved company and being in pubs. Fiddler Mikey Duggan has unforgettable memories of Sunday evenings spent in Lyons's pub, Scartaglen, with him and other musicians. Tunes would be interspersed with stories and conversation: there was nobody as good as Pádraig for keeping a group of musicians together and savouring the craic.

He shared the family home with his mother, who died in 1938, and thereafter he lived alone. He appears to have been reasonably domesticated, having a reputation of being a good baker and keeping a fairly decent table. Nor was he troubled too much by church laws of fast and abstinence. 'There are only two kinds of fast days – the day that you haven't it and the day you can't eat it,' he observed once when told that he shouldn't be eating sausages on a fast day.[4] His brother, Cal, lived in Castleisland and was devoted to him, often paying his household bills.

With the passage of time the legend of this remarkable personality continues to grow and countless anecdotes still circulate with Pádraig as the central figure. It's hard to believe that so many sayings could be attributed to one person and so many yarns told about him. In reality it is not possible that all these stories and sayings could involve him, but it can be taken that a goodly number are very much his own.

An example is the story of the parish priest who upbraided him for not being a regular attender at Sunday Mass, something which also made him a rarity in his time. ''Tis like this, father,' he is reputed to have said to the priest, 'five minutes in a church is like an hour, but an hour in a pub is like five minutes.'

Also renowned as a mimic, he could distort his face to fit another character and could change his voice to sound like a dog yelping or a lion roaring. An intelligent man, he read the newspapers and did his best to keep abreast of what was happening in the world. Though he mixed mainly with people who had far less education than himself, he also enjoyed the company of those with whom he could discuss subjects on a higher plane.

He liked to show off his command of the English language and one of the classic stories featured Pádraig responding to visits by a neighbour's trespassing donkey. Unable to sleep because of the animal's nocturnal activities, Pádraig sent the following humorous note to the owner: 'The pilfering propensities of this decrepit old animal of yours and his nightly wanderings around my residence have completely deprived me of my sleep. Therefore, if you don't remove the cause of the aforesaid disturbance, I am very reluctantly obliged to take more dramatic legal and immediate proceedings.' The owner returned the note to Pádraig forthwith with five shillings saying, 'He's worth it for that language.'[5]

Strange to relate, Pádraig didn't have a fiddle to call his own for a long period of his life, but favourite pubs, such as Lyons's and Charlie Horan's, of Castleisland, always had fiddles for him whenever he wished to play.

As he grew older, Pádraig's appearance disimproved.

People who met him for the first time in the late forties and early fifties described him as being slightly stooped, dishevelled and the worse for drink. Sadly, all available photographs of him are from that period and they graphically help tell the story of his life. Musically, he was well past his prime and wasn't as interested in playing as before. He was sixty when in 1947 he made his first radio recording with Séamus Ennis, with whom he became very friendly.

Some of the broadcasters who met him found it practically impossible to converse with him and interviews were out of the question, though he did offer a few cryptic answers to Ciarán Mac Mathúna on one occasion.

One of his best pupils, the late Jerry McCarthy, of Scartaglen, who died only a few years ago, found it hard to understand how Pádraig had become such a popular figure in the modern era:

> There were times when certain pubs were closed against him. They (the pubs) didn't want him because he was short of money and customers might feel he was looking for drink from them. There were people who looked down on him and others would leave a pub if they saw him there. But I never heard him saying anything about those people and it didn't seem to worry him.

A very rare photograph of the blind fiddler,
Tom Billy Murphy, with friends (*c*. 1930).

Denis Murphy, left front, seated alongside Seamus Ennis with friends in County Leitrim in 1948. Sean Ó Cróinín of Ballyvourney is standing at the far right. (Courtesy Julia Mary Murphy)

Pádraig O'Keeffe, the most famous of the Sliabh Luachra fiddle masters, pictured in the late 1940s. (Courtesy RTÉ)

Denis Murphy in typical playing pose. (Courtesy Julia Mary Murphy)

'Go away outa that, you devil you,' says Johnny O'Leary to Éamon Kelly.

The late Jim Thady Willie O'Connor outside his famous dance hall in Gneeveguilla several years after it closed. (Courtesy Don MacMonagle)

Mikey Duggan, of Knockrour, Scartaglen, a pupil of the late Pádraig O'Keeffe. (Courtesy Don MacMonagle)

Ciarán Mac Mathúna relaxes at home with the 'wireless'. (Courtesy RTÉ)

Another O'Keeffe pupil, Paddy Cronin of Reaboy and Killarney.
(Courtesy John Reidy)

Newmarket fiddler, archaeologist and local historian Raymond O'Sullivan.
(Courtesy Patrick Casey)

Bearded Dan Herlihy, Ballydesmond, who is collecting the old tunes of Sliabh Luachra, with Denis O'Keeffe, Rathmore. (Courtesy Patrick Casey)

Jackie Daly, one of the area's leading musicians. (Courtesy Patrick Casey)

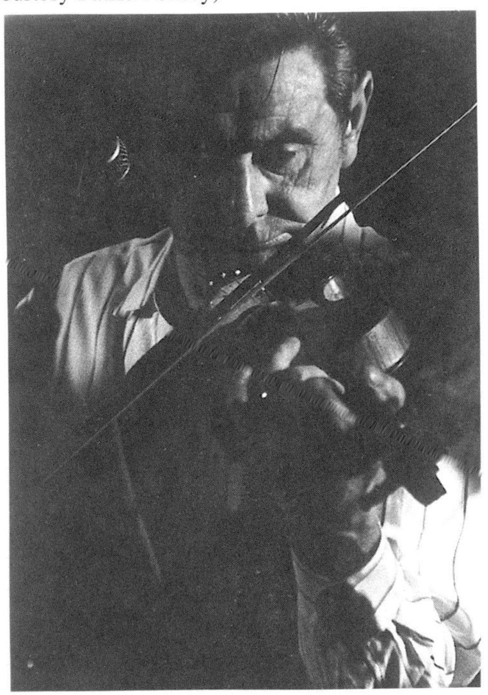

A study of Gneeveguilla fiddler Paudie Gleeson, a pupil of Pádraig O'Keeffe. (Courtesy John Reidy)

Total concentration on his music by Jimmy Doyle of Maulykeavane. (Courtesy John Reidy)

Bernard O'Donoghue, the Whitbread-Prize-winning poet who was born in Knockduff, Cullen.

The late Bridgie Kelleher and Julia Clifford, sisters of Denis Murphy, playing away into their old age. (Courtesy Don MacMonagle)

Dan O'Connell teaching Spanish students how to dance polka sets in his pub in Knocknagree during the summer of 1999. (Courtesy Patrick Casey)

Testimony to the longevity of Sliabh Luachra folk are two old-timers, Jeremiah O'Sullivan and Mike Murphy, pictured at Knocknagree Races in 1960.

The living tradition: Thomas Shine, Rockchapel, County Cork, entertains his friends. (Courtesy Patrick Casey)

Pádraig, however, still commanded the esteem of his friends in Sliabh Luachra who were always prepared to stand him a drink, or give him some money when they knew he needed it.

The harsh winter of 1962–63 was the death of Pádraig. Snow lay frozen on the ground and the steep roads around Glounthane were impassable for up to seven weeks. Those close to him had seen his appearance deteriorate for about a year before he passed away. That winter he was a virtual prisoner in his own home, but he spent a week with Tom and Mary McCarthy in their pub, at Main Street, Castleisland, in February. He was very ill and took only his usual liquid nourishment.

He made a final visit to Glounthane, driven by a neighbour, Paddy Jones. After a few days, however, his brother Cal was sent for and a doctor advised that he should be admitted to St Catherine's Hospital, in Tralee. There was a brief stop at Cordal post office for his pension and a packet of Woodbines and also at McCarthy's where, ominously, he shook hands with and bade farewell to Tom and Mary. That was unusual for him.

The feeling in the locality was that he would recover and be home again soon, but such was not to be and he died peacefully of pneumonia, on 22 February 1963, aged 75. His funeral was one of the biggest ever seen in the area and he was laid to rest in the family plot in Kilmurry graveyard.

And so one of the famous, colourful artists of Sliabh Luachra, a man who in the tradition of the poet Eoghan

Rua Ó Súilleabháin lived like an artist, had passed on. Regrettably, he was not fully acknowledged in his own lifetime. Were he to return he would surely be surprised to find that all has been put right and that he is being accorded the honour that is his due.

The music of Sliabh Luachra is now far more popular than it was in his time and it will be passed on to the future generations.

9

The Murphys – Stone Mad for Music

It has been said that only music can truly articulate the messages that come from the depths of the south-west. There are mysterious qualities in the often lonely and sometimes desolate landscape which words are inadequate to express.

If any artist gave voice to such messages it was surely Denis Murphy, one of the best loved of Sliabh Luachra musicians, both locally and nationally, and a star pupil of Pádraig O'Keeffe. His sudden death in 1974 gave rise to a huge outpouring of sorrow with the realisation that someone very rare had left the world.

In a moving tribute afterwards, Con Houlihan wrote that Denis was a man that it took generations to make.

> There is more than technical virtuosity to great art. Others were as skilled as Denis, but his genius sprang from the very rare feeling for the world that made him . . . He painted in marvellous colours, but in his music the intuition of a place and a people was like outcropping rock. You could

> smell the freshly-cut turf and see the dawn growing over Knocknaboul and hear the primeval sound of cows being driven in for milking.[1]

Denis Murphy was a member of a family that was immersed in tradition, and music was part of normal daily life at home at Lisheen, two miles from Gneeveguilla. His grandfather was a linen weaver and the Murphys became known as 'The Weavers' (the colloquial pronounciation was 'waivers'), a nickname that distinguished them from other families of the same name. All through his life Denis was known as Denis the Waiver and he sometimes got letters addressed to Denis Weaver.

The Murphys lived on a smallholding and Denis was the second youngest of eight childen born to Bill Murphy and his wife, Mary 'Mainie' Corbett, a singer of note. Bill was, in the words of one of his daughters, Julia, the youngest in the family, 'stone mad for music': he could play several instruments and was a leading member of Lisheen Fife and Drum Band.

Sessions were held regularly in the house, particularly on Sunday evenings when people would come for set dancing. 'There was music in the house morning, noon and night,' Julia told this writer in an interview many years ago.

With such a background, Denis, who was born in November 1910, could hardly avoid becoming a musician. He learned some tunes from his father and used to practise on a fiddle owned by his sister, Mary, when he had the house to himself. As he got older he and Julia would go together to Pádraig O'Keeffe's house in Glounthane for lessons.

Pádraig would also call to their house and he was the sort of individual who could arrive at any hour of the day or night. He could call at three o'clock in the morning on his way home from Knocknagree Races but he made free in houses where he was known and settled down for the night. Pádraig suited himself and might even play a few tunes before sleeping off the effects of drink.

Julia Murphy had a remarkably sharp ear for music and was very good at picking up tunes by listening carefully. In her old age (she lived well into her eighties), she used tell of how a man known as Danny Ab would visit her home when she was a child. Danny would whistle tunes whilst in the house and Julia would later play them on her fiddle. There's a tune still in circulation called 'Danny Ab's'.

All the Murphy children played. Most of them emigrated and Dan is remembered as an excellent fiddler who performed in New York in dance halls and on radio with the great musicians of the 1920s and '30s, such as Paddy Killoran and James Morrison.

At home, meanwhile, the services of the younger Murphys were in demand for the usual dances and house parties and Denis and Julia frequently played with the likes of Pádraig O'Keeffe, Din Tarrant, Dan O'Leary and Johnny O'Leary.

Johnny O'Leary, who later formed a brilliant combination with Denis Murphy, has never forgotten a visit to Lisheen in the late 1940s, when he witnessed a session involving Bill Murphy, Denis, Julia and a neighbour, John Clifford, who married Julia.

Cupid entered Denis Murphy's life when he started courting Julia Mary Sheehan of Tureencahill, a few miles away, and they were married in 1942. During the war years, Denis would cut turf and sell it, but there wasn't very much doing after the war and he and Julia emigrated to New York in 1949. Between three different visits, the couple spent ten years in the US and worked in a variety of everyday jobs in restaurants, the railway, Bronx Zoo, the New York Botanical Gardens and Fordham University. The last job Denis had was at Columbia University where on a conferring day he once danced a hornpipe on a makeshift stage as a workmate whistled, much to the amusement of gowned graduates and professors who stopped for a look.

During his time in America Denis met and played with numerous leading musicians such as Andy McGann, Paddy Killoran and Lad O'Beirne. He also made 78 rpm records whilst there. Even though the Murphys enjoyed their time in America, they never intended staying there permanently. Denis didn't like the humidity of New York and joked that he often longed for a cooling shower of rain that he would have been so familiar with at home.

Always anxious for news from Kerry, he and fellow-musician Jerry McCarthy, from Scartaglen, once met a newcomer to the Big Apple and took him to a bar. They were settling down for an evening's chat about life back home when the sound of gunfire rang out. Their guest became alarmed and asked what it was all about. Denis, displaying typical wit, declared, 'I don't know, but 'tis hardly a fox they're firing at.' A story which shows that his heart was always at home.

Denis and Julia Mary finally returned to Ireland in 1965 and a built a bungalow for themselves in Lisheen. They were happy to be released from the hurly-burly of New York and soon settled into a leisurely lifestyle at home. Denis attended fleadhanna cheoil, meeting up with old friends, and he also became friendly with Seán Ó Riada, who loved his music.

Once, after a long Saturday night playing music in Seán Ó Riada's home in Coolea, Denis and others were a bit late heading up the road for Sunday Mass. When someone urged the group to hurry, the ever humorous Denis irreverently replied, 'Ah sure we'll make the hornpipe [last part of the polka set] anyway!'

Standing over six feet and built accordingly, Denis was a fine cut of a man with good looks and black wavy hair. He and Julia Mary were a striking couple as they walked into Gneeveguilla chapel on Sunday mornings with that unmistakable, swanky American look, he in a check jacket and smartly-pressed pants and she elegantly attired in the fashion of the day. They stood out in times when clothes worn by country people were plain, dark and all looked the same. But Denis and Julia were still Sliabh Luachra folk to the marrow of their bones, as one realised when they spoke – with no trace of an American accent.

Significantly, at this time Dan O'Connell's pub in Knocknagree started to become a venue for set dancing, with Denis and Johnny O'Leary providing the music – an arrangement that was to last for nine hectic years until the untimely death of Denis, on 7 April 1974, after he came home from his usual Sunday night session in Dan O'Connell's. He was sixty-three.

There was something uncanny about his last night playing in O'Connell's. That night he did things differently. As usual, he was partnered by Johnny O'Leary. 'Denis played fourteen or fifteen tunes I'd never heard before, jigs, reels and slides and he told me he'd give them to me the next night. I hadn't a note of any of those tunes,' said Johnny.[2]

Tears still come to Dan O'Connell's eyes when he recalls Denis Murphy's final session and driving him home to Lisheen afterwards.

> Himself and Art (Aut) O'Keeffe played for about half an hour, or three-quarters of an hour, outside the door when the usual night's music was finished inside. That was something Denis never did before. He and Aut played a variety of old marching tunes from Lisheen and the crowd stayed on listening to them. I took him home

> and I remember as we passed Lisheen Cross we were talking about music. I left him home at around a quarter past twelve and couldn't believe it when I heard the following morning that he had died during the night.

His death shocked the world of traditional music and there was a huge attendance at his funeral in Gneeve-guilla.

It's difficult to find anyone with a bad word to say about Denis Murphy, who is usually described as a *grámhar* (lovable), laid-back, fun-loving man and an absolutely gifted musician with a huge repertoire. The look of total concentration on his face as he played showed how involved he was in the music, but he was a light-hearted and witty individual by nature. Julia Mary says she never heard him saying anything ugly about anyone: he was a very gentle man who hated commotion and always wanted things to run smoothly.

According to Dan O'Connell, Denis had an uplifting effect on people and was always associated with fun and enjoyment. 'No matter how sorry, or down and out you'd be, meeting him would always lift you.'

Music was his whole life. He used to say that the sound made when he opened a certain gate in his own place was the first bar of the 'Cualann'. Even while travelling in the car Julia Mary could guess what type of tune he was thinking about by the speed at which he was driving.

Fellow musicians and broadcasters were always assured of a hearty welcome in Lisheen, with the likes of Séamus Ennis and Ivor Browne, both from Dublin, being regular callers. Sessions could go all day and all night in the Murphy home, while fields of hay were often abandoned in the cause of music. A story is told of how Denis received a letter one morning asking him to meet Seán Mac Réamoinn, of RTÉ, at Rathmore railway station. A builder had been engaged by Denis for that day and was working away when the postman arrived with the letter from Mac Réamoinn. Mortar had been mixed and Denis was set for a day's work, but he had to go to meet Mac Réamoinn and that was the end of building work for that day and a day or two after.

Unlike Pádraig O'Keeffe, Denis made many recordings. He was also luckier than O'Keeffe in other ways: Ireland began to improve economically during his lifetime and the music had become more popular than it had been in the O'Keeffe era.

Some people, including Julia Mary, maintain that Denis played his best music in quiet places with only close friends present, a phenomenon that is true of many musicians. But his recordings reflect his unique gifts. A CD and cassette produced by Peter Browne of RTÉ twenty years after his death contains twenty-three tunes that were recorded between 1948 and 1969 by Séamus Ennis, Ciarán Mac Mathúna and Aindrias Ó Gallachóir.

People have described Denis Murphy's playing in

various ways – 'a great bowhand . . . nice light fingers, supple, relaxed and he never got tied up in a tune . . . used to take the last note of a phrase and belt it into the start of the next phrase which gave it great lift and excitement.'[3]

He played all types of tunes and was known for the way he would play 'The Blackbird' and dance at the same time. His lively, happy personality was transmitted through the music and he always got a great kick out of playing slides and polkas for good dancers.

Denis Murphy was sometimes criticised for not teaching the music to young people, but his friend Dan O'Connell argues that the musician did his bit to hand on the music. Says O'Connell, 'There are two ways of teaching music – one by holding classes, the other by sitting down and playing with young musicians and telling them all you know, giving them tips and bits of advice. Denis was brilliant at teaching the second way and he loved to play with younger musicians who were attracted by his warm personality.'

Growing up in Lisheen, the Murphys taught each other music. From an early age, Julia saw her father and siblings, Thady, Dan and Mary, playing together. When they put the fiddles aside she would take one up and it was Thady who taught her the first tune. Julia picked up tunes more by ear than by reading notes and became an accomplished player. Denis once conceded that she could perform more tricks with fiddle strings than he could. She emigrated to Scotland and later went to London where she became an established musician in a number of bands with her husband, John Clifford. On returning to Ireland in the 1950s, the Cliffords formed their own highly-rated band, The Star of Munster, before going back to London in 1958. The band made several recordings and the Cliffords' son, Billy, who now lives in Tipperary, is a splendid concert flute player.

Julia won the senior fiddle competition at the 1963 All-Ireland Fleadh Cheoil and Billy won the title for concert flute in 1970. (Denis, by the way, had a strong dislike of competitions.)

The eldest of the Murphy family, Bridgie (Mrs Kelleher), who took up the concertina at an early age, remained at home all her life. She once played a tune on the fiddle in Dan O'Connell's at the age of ninety-two and lived to be just two years short of a century.

The 'Waivers' didn't have much material wealth, but, culturally, they were a rich family. And as well as being natural musicians they were extremely likeable people, as summed up by Con Houlihan in his farewell to Denis:

> I feel about Denis as Patrick Kavanagh did in the wonderful lines about his mother. I do not think of him lying in the dark earth of Gneeveguilla graveyard. He is seated in a pub kitchen; the fire is bright and his fiddle is singing; he is telling one of his wildly irreverent stories and the spring of his laughter is bubbling; he and his wife are

welcoming you into their house and making you feel as if you were the first citizen of the world. And you smile at us eternally.

10

Johnny O'Leary
Custodian of the Music

He's the living legend of Sliabh Luachra, a vital link in the chain of tradition. Johnny O'Leary (known to one and all as Johnny Leary) is special in many ways and he was once described by the late, renowned collector of Irish music, Breandán Breathnach, as the 'national custodian' of the music of the area.

As well as being a gifted performer, he has inherited much local history and folkore and is a natural yarn-spinner. He cracks jokes between tunes about the characters of other days, going into convulsions at times. The best of company and a laugh-a-minute man, his language is earthy and his colourful speech gushes forth like the flooded cascades in the Owenacree river not far from his birthplace.

Today, this outgoing, friendly personality who exudes the lively spirit of his birthplace is more sought-after than ever and is as well known at sessions in haunts like Moran's Hotel and the Piper's Club in Dublin, as he is in the 'rushy mountain': testimony to the popularity of his music. There's sheer joy in every note he fingers and a sense of unbridled gaiety fills the air.

Johnny was born in Maulykevane (also known as Jib), west of Gneeveguilla, in June 1923, and music was all around him from his cradle days. At that time, the fiddle was the most popular instrument but he fell upon an accordeon more or less by accident. An uncle, Patie, had purchased the 'box' in Clancy's, Killarney, for 12/6 (62.5 pence). Another uncle, Dan, was handy on the fiddle and Patie had notions about himself being a good player too.

Such was not to be but Patie guarded his ten-key, three-stopper accordeon jealously and wouldn't let Johnny, who showed an interest from the age of five or six, near it at first. Whenever Patie left the house Johnny would take it down and start to play. The youngster was caught on a few occasions, with Patie nearly pulling the two ears off him, but Patie eventually gave in and Johnny, who went on to take lessons from Pádraig O'Keeffe, kept on playing. Johnny began to play with his Uncle Dan, an accomplished musician, and they were joined at times by Denis and Julia Murphy. Encouragement came from John Clifford who, memorably, once told Johnny that he was a good player and would continue to improve.

He had the knack of picking up a tune quickly and could easily retain it, just by thinking about it while lying in bed the night he'd hear it. He reckons that after almost seventy years of playing music he has up to

1,500 tunes stored away in his computer-like brain. And many of them were never christened. 'Some tunes I don't know I have at all till I hear someone else playing them. Then they come back to me. 'Tis amazing.'

He had the distinction of having a book, featuring 384 of his tunes collected by Breandán Breathnach and Terry Moylan, published in 1994.[1] Collection work is continuing and it is hoped to publish more of his tunes.

Since boyhood, Johnny has been gathering tunes wherever he goes. Older musicians like Pádraig O'Keeffe, Bill 'The Waiver' Murphy, Jack Connell, Jack Sweeney and Joe Conway were fruitful sources. So extensive was the repertoire of the district that he was hearing new tunes all the time. 'Twould frighten you. There was no end at all to some of the old fellows. Every night I'd go some place, I'd hear tunes I never heard before and many of the musicians playing them would hardly ever have left their own townland.'

When he was learning he'd put the accordeon on his back in all weathers and walk the eight or nine miles to Scartaglen to meet Pádraig O'Keeffe, generally in Jack Lyons's pub. He'd return home with a few new tunes and, by making repeat visits, gradually built up his own repertoire. Even before he entered his teens, he was playing for sets at Toremore Hall with seasoned players like Jack Sweeney and Jackie Fleming, joined on occasions by Denis Murphy and Mick O'Mahony (Quarry Cross).

It was Mick O'Mahony who gave him the start to a

partnership with Denis Murphy that was to last all of thirty-eight years and ended prematurely with the sudden death of Denis in 1974. One night Mick was due to play with Denis in Thady Willie's hall in Gneeveguilla, but was unable to fulfill the engagement. Johnny, then only thirteen, was called on to sit in for him. He played many a night thereafter in Thady Willie's and in countless venues with Denis Murphy. In those days Johnny also took an interest in Sligo musicians such as Michael Coleman and James Morrison and bought some of Coleman's 78 rpm records which he played over and over again.

When Johnny was growing up he was often asked to play at house dances and thoroughly enjoyed himself. He was also a regular at pattern days and Sunday-evening crossroad dances. When dance halls became more popular in the thirties he was in demand at halls all around the district.

Whenever he thinks of Pádraig O'Keeffe, one of his main influences, he chuckles, rubs his brow and stories begin to flow . . . did you hear this one, or that one? 'Pádraig was nearly always short of money and he got a "weakness"once in Lyons's pub, but a drop of brandy brought him round. A few more drinks followed and when one of the prime boys tried to get one of the drinks from Pádraig what did he tell him only to go away and get a weakness of his own.'

According to Johnny, Pádraig was a genius but like many another artist had a failing for drink. He needed a few before playing, but couldn't play at all when he had too many and wasn't inclined to play much during the last few years of his life. Johnny also respected Pádraig's judgement of a musician. He taught hundreds of pupils, the odd one brilliant, some good, a few fair and others downright poor.

Johnny made the first of his many radio recordings with Séamus Ennis, in 1947, and he vividly remembers the occasion at the Murphys' old house, in Lisheen. Denis and Julia were there, as was their father, Bill, an old man at the time but still well able to play. 'I remember Bill putting his hand behind a curtain and bringing out a concert flute with a big cobweb stuck on to it. Ennis told him to wipe away the cobweb but Bill said no, claiming the music would be all the sweeter if he left it where it was. He played away and 'twas beautiful music.'

To this day Johnny still feels a little nervous prior to a live radio recording and relaxes with a half-glass of whiskey. As for television appearances, he has a definite dislike of the screen. 'They'd all be watching, you know. The critics, I mean, would be remarking on your playing.' What's more he believes television militates against the music, as the goggle-box in the corner now comes first in most houses.[2] In his youth, there was an instrument in nearly every home and people loved a few hours of music to pass away the time.

There's nothing he likes better than playing in a pub: he savours the atmosphere and regards himself as a musician for dancers, with a definite preference for sets. He still gets a buzz from seeing people enjoying his dance music. He brings the best out of them and they out of him. A modern-day Sliabh Luachra poet, Dónal Ó Síodhcháin, wrote of him:

Bringing his dancers with him,
Feet belting off the floor,
Faces bright as their Kerry slide
And round they go once more.

Johnny has played regularly in Dan O'Connell's since 1965. It is unquestionably his favourite venue and he never misses a chance to hand out bouquets to O'Connell for his contribution to the popularity of traditional music, set dancing in particular. 'Not only has Dan provided a welcome place for musicians to play in, he has also made fine facilities available for dancers. I've hardly seen a place where dancing and music go together so well.'

Whatever about his liking for Knocknagree Johnny still rates Gneeveguilla as the home of Sliabh Luachra music. He observes that for a small place it has produced a remarkable number of richly-talented musicians. 'Give me Denis Murphy and Julia; Bill Larry O'Sullivan and the brothers, Paddy and Johnny Cronin, and I guarantee you wouldn't get any five musicians in any area in Ireland to better them. I'd take them anywhere.'

Intensely proud of his musical heritage, Johnny is always generous about sharing his knowledge and takes pride in having started two talented musicians on the road, a near neighbour Jimmy Doyle and Liam Browne, a native of Barraduff who is now in the restaurant business in New York. Johnny's wife, Lil (née Kelly), who comes from Gullane, Gneeveguilla, is a lover of the music and a cousin of the actor and seanchaí Éamon Kelly. The couple, who live in Rathmore, have a grown-up family of three, Ellen, Maureen and Seán. The only one of the O'Leary children to take to music is Ellen, who's a fine tin whistle player. Maureen can also play while Seán is far more interested in football.

All through his long life Johnny, who worked in Cadbury's chocolate factory, Rathmore, has never stopped learning. Collectors are fascinated by the surprises he continues to throw up. He has played with musicians from many places with varying styles and has made several long-playing records and tapes. Fellow musicians have given to him and he to them.

In an introduction to *Johnny O'Leary of Sliabh Luachra*, Terry Moylan wrote:

> One of the amazing things I encountered when collecting his music was that there was no fall-off in the relative incidence of new items. There was no 'diminishing return' effect. A night of playing for sets in August 1993 yielded some two dozen unheard-of tunes and that experience was typical.

Writing in *Ceol* (1981), Breandán Breathnach observed:

> Johnny has retained the push-and-draw method of the old-fashioned melodeon and he uses that system with fine effect to articulate the music . . . To satisfy the dancers in Kerry, the music must be played fast and strong, and speed and vigour are features of Johnny's playing. But he is always in control and the sustained pulse and forward thrust which are noticeable in his music makes dancing compulsive for his listeners.

Cork musician Con Ó Drisceoil believes that Johnny has all the attributes necessary for a good box-player: a large and varied repertoire, a strong, infectious rhythm, an energetic approach to dance music and an ability to bring out the best in a tune through good ornamentation and variation.

One of the best tributes to Johnny comes from a musician who has played with him over a lifetime, Mikey Duggan, who says that Johnny's style is the nearest to Pádraig O'Keeffe's that he knows.

The years have been kind to ageless Johnny, who's full of roguery and devilment. They still can't get enough of him and his likes may not be seen again.

11

THE SINGING TRADITION

Traditional (*sean-nós*) singing with 'come all ye' style songs is often parodied by people who have no idea of what it's about, nor the slightest appreciation of what's involved. But such singing is an art form in its own right and very much part of Sliabh Luachra's musical heritage.

Another false impression is that all traditional songs are sad. Nothing could be further from the truth: some are bubbling over with laughter. This kind of singing is an art which comes straight from the cabin fireside. The songs are penned by local people drawing inspiration from local happenings and aimed at small, intimate audiences who know exactly what the song and the singer are all about.

When called upon to sing the singer is often a bit shy and needs some persuasion. Eventually yielding, the throat is cleared and the first notes come. You can hear a proverbial pin drop as the story in song begins.

In olden times, songs were learned on a mother's knee, in rambling houses, at ball nights and station dances, or purchased in the form of penny ballad sheets from street singers at fairs in Knocknagree. I vividly remember the late Timmy Jer O'Connor of Gneeveguilla returning from fairs, sitting down with his stockinged feet toasting by an open fire and singing song after song from the crumpled sheets. Spailpíns returning from their work in Limerick and Cork, as well as soldiers coming home from wars in France and Flanders, also brought new songs into the area which always aroused keen interest and were added to, or adapted to suit, the local repertoire.

What makes traditional singer is difficult to define because the art is a very individual, flexible one with no strict set of rules. The singer must communicate with the audience and identify with the song. A good ear is essential and, in true traditional fashion, the young can learn an amount from older practitioners.

Jimmy O'Brien has for many years been one of Sliabh Luachra's best known singers and he learned much from his late uncle, Paddy Coakley, who lived in Glenflesk. Paddy had hundreds of songs, some of which were collected from him and from Jimmy by Tom Mullaney of the Folklore Commission and safely stored away in the national archives.

According to Jimmy, a singer must have a personal style which comes from listening to older singers and carefully studying their ornamentation and variation, though not copying them. 'You hear them and take careful note. Unconsciously it sinks into you but it could take weeks, or months, before the penny drops and you then sing the song perfectly in your own style . . . '

When in the peak of form, a singer can gave an enthralling performance, but if you asked him to sing the same song and in the same way a half an hour later, he couldn't repeat it exactly. He won't sing a song in the same manner twice. A traditional singer, nearly always without musical accompaniment, has plenty of freedom to treat a song in his own way and can be totally unpredictable.

Styles and techniques vary from place to place. Even two singers from the same townland can take a completely different approach to a song. The story is always important and that's why a singer will render every verse right to the end, no matter how long the song might be. Some singers focus on projecting the story whilst others are more concerned with the musical aspects, embellishment and variation. They sing in phrases and the last few words are often spoken in a casual, throwaway fashion rather than sung.

Years ago in Sliabh Luachra, well before radio and television were heard of, there were scores of singers who weren't tops musically but who could hold an audience spellbound by dramatically concentrating on the theme of a song and delivering it with passion. Jimmy O'Brien and most other experts believe that there's no better setting than a country kitchen or a small hall for a traditional singer. A pub is not always an ideal venue as singers generally prefer not to use amplification and it can be difficult to be heard over the din of a noisy crowd of drinkers.

Feeling for a song is also vital. A singer when relating the story of an ambush, for instance, can act as if in the thick of battle himself. This feeling is conveyed most effectively to a small audience sitting around him. The exuberant Paddy Doyle has few equals when it comes to doing just that with heart and gusto.

Songs about emigration were guaranteed to get tears flowing at, say, an American wake and people were moved by lyrics like 'Shall I no more gaze on the shore' – the last thoughts of a young emigrant who would in all probability never see Ireland again – taken from one of the area's most famous songs, 'Sweet Kingwilliamstown' (the old name for Ballydesmond). Local man Danny Buckley, who survived the Titanic disaster but was killed on the last day of World War I, has always been credited with writing this song, though some people dispute his authorship.

In any case it's a classic traditional song which has long since become part of the national repertoire and few people can sing it as well as the Clare maestro Séamus Mac Mathúna when in top form:

My bonny barque bounced light and free
Across the surging foam
Which bears me far from Innisfail
To seek a foreign home.
A lonely exile driven 'neath
Misfortune's coldest frown

From my loved home and cherished friends
In dear Kingwilliamstown.

Similar emotions were evoked by the following lines from 'The Green Hills of Kerry':

At eight in the morning, my train will be starting,
And I'll be torn from all I love best
How sad and how lonely will then be my parting
When I'll bid adieu saying I'm bound for the west.

There were songs which brought laughter and hilarity to proceedings. Characters who could sing funny songs like 'The Taglioni', or 'Brian O'Lynn', were plentiful in the area. They would lilt the chorus whilst dancing over a brush, belting it out on the floor with dust rising. Italian in origin, the taglioni was a long, multi-purpose overcoat worn almost to the ankles and it came into Ireland after World War I As well as being a garment that gave protection against the elements, it was also known to serve as a blanket, or a groundsheet, for courting couples.

The following is a verse from 'The Taglioni':

With a skating party I did go, myself no skating master,
And as I skated on the ice, I met with great disaster
And as I skated on the ice, it being thin and stoney
The ice it bent and in I went and wet my taglioni.

Paddy Coakley nearly went to America as a young man, but as he was about to board a liner in Cobh his papers were found to be not in order and he was turned back. That was a lucky stroke for traditional singing because Paddy, who had a song for every day of the year, passed on many of his songs. He married into the Fleming family of Glenflesk, who were also musical.

Paddy learnt his singing from his mother, Bessy Ryan, and the tradition has been handed down the family line with Siobhán O'Brien-Rae, Jimmy's daughter, about to pass it on to a fifth generation. She is a splendid singer and winner of numerous competitions, including an under-18 Oireachtas award.

It would be impossible to name all the fine singers that Sliabh Luachra has produced, but two, Joan Murphy and Hannah (Han) Dennehy (née Cronin), both now sadly deceased, came to national prominence in the 1950s and '60s through Radio Éireann broadcasts. Joan, a nurse in St Finan's Hospital, Killarney, hailed from Clonkeen and her interpretation of 'The Rocks of Bawn' was acclaimed as one of the best. Unfortunately, she died while still in her prime. Han, a member of the talented Cronin family from Reaboy, Gneeveguilla, married Mick Dennehy, of Couneragh, Rathmore. Blessed with a powerful, distinct voice she is well remembered for her stirring treatment of 'The Shores of Amerikay'.

The end of house dances was a serious blow to traditional singing, which is not now as popular in Sliabh

Luachra as formerly. Some exponents, however, can still command audiences – like Jerry Kelly or the sweet-voiced Mary Lenihan, of Ballydesmond, a singer who always projects a love of her art and is assured of a welcome wherever traditionalists gather, to mention just two.

Of the younger generation, Margaret Counihan, of Tournanough, Gneeveguilla, and Patrice O'Connor of Kilcummin, stand out as artists worthy of the tradition they're inheriting. Both girls have been very successful in competitions.

Christy Cronin is one of the area's leading male singers and he got some of his songs from his late father, Pat Thady Mick, also an excellent singer. These songs are mainly about local events, tragedies such as the moving bog disaster, heroes, love, emigration, townlands and villages, ambushes and sport. It's the air of a song that first attracts Christy, who also likes verses which rhyme well. Born in January 1943, he soon discovered his musical ear as songs were frequently sung at his home in Maughantourig, about a mile west of Gneeveguilla, when the day's farmwork was done. He was also inspired by the singing of the choir in Gneeveguilla chapel and by singers in local pubs and Knocknagree fair.[1]

Christy fondly remembers the singers of his youth, people from whom he got some of the songs he sings today – Timmy 'Tailor' Cahill, D. D. Cronin, Nellie Keane, Mike Cronin (Reaboy), Tom Cronin, Arthur

O'Keeffe, Pat Buckley, Andy and Paddy Sheehan and the Cronin twins from Raheen, who could sing in amazing harmony.

When he has a song off by heart Christy goes about ornamenting it, giving it his own personal touch. He believes that ornamentation is a big part of the art of singing; either a singer has it, or he hasn't. Silence is also very important as a singer has to be able to hear himself and to create an atmosphere. 'I enjoy nothing better than a session with four, or five, people involved, each giving a song in turn. That's what it's all about.'

A pleasant, easy-going man, Christy has made a huge number of radio recordings. He loves being asked to sing and is always in demand for concerts, house parties and other functions in the area. He has long since lost count of the number of songs he has collected, many of which are from other parts of the country.

Some of his songs are full of sentiment and a favourite of his own is 'The Charming Quarry Cross' which opens as follows:

One evening fair to take the air I strayed from my abode
I quickly passed by Tureenamult Cross along the quarry road,
My mind it being unoccupied as I wandered in a dream
Till awakened by the rippling of the quarry mountain stream
With open eyes and much surprise around me I did gaze,

To view the scenes of meadows green I stood in deep
amaze
The heather brown was gaily crowned like a wreath o'er
the dew wet moss
With such beauty rare none can compare with the
charming Quarry Cross.

That song was written many years ago by a local songsmith who signed himself 'Island Bard'. There was no shortage of local poets and songwriters in the area and the poems were often converted into songs. To this day, songwriters emerge whenever a major football victory, or any occasion of note, needs to be celebrated in verse. Christy Cronin, who has won eight Kerry county championship medals for singing, has a number of superb, all-Irish songs, including 'An Áit úd Claodach ina Rugadh mé', which he got from a close friend, the late Frank Cronin, who died all too young.[2]

Claodach (Clydagh) is a mountain valley on the southern side of the Paps and a place where Irish was spoken well into the present century. The song tells of the wild beauty of Claodach, of mountain streams, of sweet songbirds and nature's glories:

Ós mo chóir 'na seasamh
Bhi radharc gan easnamh,
An dá Chic Dannain go hard sa spéir
Ag déanamh garda don gleann go léir . . . '

[There standing in front of me,
There was a sight without blemish,
The two Paps high in the sky
Guarding the whole glen.]

12

Collectors and Broadcasters

Ciarán Mac Mathúna jokes that he never has any trouble in reaching Gneeveguilla through a maze of wending roads in the dark, but he might find it difficult enough in daylight.

He has been coming to Sliabh Luachra since the 1950s, doing, as he says himself, a job of journeywork . . . collecting music. In the old days that work was usually done at night and in winter: it was convenient for the local people to do recordings at night; being generally farming folk, they were at their leisure when days were short and evenings long.

Long before local people realised what a wealth of traditional music they had, collectors saw Sliabh Luachra as a storehouse of its own special brand of *ceol* and the collectors made a major contribution, not only in bringing that ceol to a national audience but also in helping to heighten respect for it within Sliabh Luachra.

Mac Mathúna, the silver-haired radio voice of traditional music, has maintained close links with the area for almost half a century. But another of the distinguished collectors, Séamus Ennis, got to Sliabh Luachra before Ciarán. Séamus, also a singer and piper of note, was amongst the early collectors to come, arriving in the mid-1940s, and was employed for some time by the BBC.

Word about Sliabh Luachra music and Pádraig O'Keeffe, in particular, began to get out in the late 1930s and the Ó Cróinín brothers, Seán and Donncha, from the Gaeltacht area of Ballyvourney, County Cork, were most likely the first to arrive. Seán used basic equipment for field recording and it was from Donncha that Séamus Ennis heard about Pádraig.

One of the first musicians from the area to make a radio broadcast was the young John Clifford, of Lisheen, who got on Radio Éireann whilst on a trip home from London around 1939–40. John made four radio appearances in a short period and he often told of how on one occasion he and Denis Murphy cycled from Lisheen to the studios in Cork and home again that night, a round journey of a hundred miles.

There was a significant broadcasting breakthrough around 1947 when Radio Éireann introduced mobile recording units which enabled collectors to go out and record music on location. Farmhouse kitchens and back rooms of pubs became improvised studios. Prior to that recordings had to be made in conventional radio studios.

Séamus Ennis, a Dubliner, first met Pádraig O'Keeffe during Easter 1946 in Jack Lyons's pub, Scartaglen, a favourite haunt of Pádraig. The meeting was arranged by the Ó Cróinín brothers. Denis Murphy was also there and a memorable night's music resulted, with four fiddlers and Séamus on the pipes.

'I had heard so much about Pádraig from Donncha (Ó Cróinín) that I felt compelled to go and see him and I can tell you I wasn't disappointed,' Séamus recalled many years later.[1]

> The shop was a long, narrow one going back from the door and there was a large room on the left with a big open hearth and a roaring fire, by the side of which Pádraig sat complete with a fiddle and two pints of stout on a mantle shelf above him. Well, he had a great welcome for us and wasn't a bit daunted by the presence of clergy who bore the brunt of many a wily jest before the night was out.

Chairs and boxes were provided for the visitors and plain porter dispensed. It was then that the strangers noted Pádraig's peculiar manner of drinking a pint. With the first sup he emptied the glass down to this thumb, 'below the chapel windows', as he used to say, and never took another drink from it until the next creamy pint was landed safely beside it.

A couple of young Tipperary brothers, the Clancys, who were later to become famous for their ballad singing in America, visited Sliabh Luachra in the early 1950s with the American collector Diane Hamilton and she, too, recorded Pádraig in Lyons's pub. She admired his light, agile, flowing style and later wrote, 'His fiddle was kept hanging on a nail over the counter. The hairs for the bow he had recently pulled from a horse's tail. They were tied in a large knot at the top and held away from the wood by the cork of a stout bottle.'

Other collectors to go to the area included Aindreas Ó Gallachóir, Breandán Breathnach, Séan Mac Réamoinn and Prionsias Ó Conluain. Ciarán Mac Mathúna, however, stands head and shoulders over everybody else as a broadcaster of the music. Born in Limerick city in November 1925, he grew up surrounded by music as his father was a teacher with a vast repertoire of traditional airs. Ciarán took a degree in Irish at University College, Dublin, and later completed an MA thesis on the themes of Irish folk songs.

After working for a while with the Irish Placenames Commission he joined the Radio Éireann mobile unit in 1954. The unit wanted a music specialist to help record traditional material as part of a brief to capture every aspect of rural Ireland on tape and the Shannon-sider was an ideal choice. Ciarán went about his task with cool, controlled enthusiasm and headed out into the highways and byways. The mobile unit was a key advantage in that musicians could be recorded in the relaxed setting of their own homes, in pubs and halls: all this was in contrast to the more formal, technical atmosphere of a studio which had intimidating microphones and cables all around the place. As well as that, the natural setting added to the authenticity of the recordings. The late Johnny Spillane of Glenflesk was sound engineer for several of the recordings and was a great help to Ciarán, for he knew the people and didn't need a road map to find his way around Sliabh Luachra. The pair travelled many miles together.

At that time, a visit by a recording unit always generated excitement and anticipation. Musicians who were scarcely known outside their own areas were offered the rare glory of being heard on the national airwaves. Following such broadcasts, bands and some individual performers advertised themselves as being of 'radio fame'.

A week or two in advance of the visit, the postman would bring a letter from Ciarán to a contact person. Musicians, singers and dancers would then be alerted and all were guaranteed to turn up punctually at a house, or pub, on the appointed evening. A decent crowd was always assured, with loads of encouragement for the performers, most of whom would be making their début on air a short time later. Recordings might start around suppertime and sessions could go on all night, often until five or six o'clock in the morning.

On the evening of the actual broadcast cows would be milked early and a deal of stowing done around the house. A good fire would be set with everyone, neighbours included, gathering round it. Not a word would be uttered as a local artist performed on air, just nods and winks of approval, and a session would invariably follow in the kitchen for the remainder of the night.

Mac Mathúna first met and recorded Denis Murphy

at a feis in Kenmare in the summer of 1956. The occasion marked the beginning of a long friendship and the broadcaster's first of many recordings of Denis at the Murphy home in Lisheen also took place that year.

At the Kenmare session he also recorded a young musician, Cornelius (Con) O'Sullivan, son of Peter C. and Mrs O'Sullivan of Banard, Gneeveguilla. Con was an American citizen who was brought to Ireland as a youngster by his parents. A protégé of Denis Murphy, he was a talented fiddler and Ciarán got to know him well when he was a medical student at UCD. Con qualified as a doctor and returned to the US, where he has lived for many years.

Ciarán's first meeting with Pádraig O'Keeffe was also in 1956. Though past his best at the time, the maestro could still play good music and had an astounding repertoire. Pádraig was not an easy man to interview and, as Ciarán humorously recalled many years later, was not too anxious to talk to a 'little whippersnapper like myself.' When he asked Pádraig where Glounthane was, the reply was brief: 'Where the bog is.'

It was with Denis Murphy that Ciarán formed the closest bonds. The musician often stayed in the Mac Mathúna family home when he went to Dublin to play.

> Denis never took himself seriously, but he took his music very seriously. The fiddle was part of him. Nobody will ever know the full extent of his repertoire and when I first met him he played a

> few tunes he had no name for. He would play music at any hour of the day, or night. It was his whole life.[2]

They did other recordings at Jack Lyons's, Scartaglen, with Pádraig O'Keeffe, Denis and musicians such as Dan Cronin and Johnny O'Leary. Ciarán also recorded Denis with Jerry McCarthy of Scartaglen in America in the 1960s.

Though he used to joke about keeping the 'gander's neck' (microphone) away from him, Denis had no hang-ups about recording, or about anything for that matter, and didn't mind where he played. Another technological advance, the portable tape recorder, made life easier for collectors and was less off-putting for the artists they recorded.

In the course of a series of retrospective radio programmes on RTÉ produced by Harry Bradshaw following Ciarán's retirement in 1990, the legendary broadcaster related an hilarious incident involving himself and Jerry McCarthy in the late 1950s:

> We were travelling from Castleisland to Feoghanagh, in South Limerick, on a very bad, dark and rainy night in November. Jerry was playing the fiddle as we went along in the car when all of a sudden and out of nowhere emerged a black cow. We hit the cow, or the cow hit us.
>
> We got out of the car and Jerry was giving out

> to the man driving the cow in the middle of the night with no light. But the cow shook herself and was alright . . . the only damage was to the headlight of my car. But worse than that, Jerry had forgotten that he had left the fiddle on the passenger seat. He sat on top of it when he got back in and that was the end of the fiddle.

While on recording trips to Sliabh Luachra, the Radio Éireann crew based themselves in Killarney where publican Jimmy O'Brien was a well-informed contact. The first recording in O'Brien's took place soon after he opened the pub in 1961 and O'Brien says that it was one of the very rare times in his long career when he stayed open after hours.

Another session that Ciarán has fond memories of took place in the home of schoolteacher Denny Spillane, a brother of the aforementioned Johnny, in Glenflesk. The session went on all day and Ciarán met some of the younger Sliabh Luachra musicians for the first time, like Liam Browne of Barraduff, now in New York, and the late Joan Murphy, who sang some beautiful songs.

Artists such as Seán Ó Riada, living on the other side of the Paps in Coolea, and Ceoltóirí Cualann, who helped popularise Irish traditional music in the 1960s, also drew inspiration from the music and musicians of Sliabh Luachra, sometimes sharing broadcasting studios with them.

RTÉ is often criticised for allegedly not giving

enough time to Irish music but in fairness the station has, since the 1940s, collected and recorded a vast amount of music which now forms an invaluable archive. Broadcasts on radio through programmes like *Ballad-makers' Saturday Night*, *A Job of Journeywork*, *Ceolta Tíre*, *Céilí House* and *Mo Cheol Thú*, to mention a few, brought the music to a national audience and played a vital role in promoting the cultural treasures of Sliabh Luachra. The work of broadcasters has contributed immeasurably to the preservation of the music and to bringing it to the lofty position it enjoys today.

In more recent times local radio has also been willing to give airtime to musicians and cater for the large audience that the music now attracts. Using modern technology it is now possible to reproduce in CD and cassette form recordings which have lain for many years in dusty archives. The first, featuring the music of Pádraig O'Keeffe, was produced by RTÉ's Peter Browne in 1993. Another followed in 1994, this time with the music of Denis Murphy. Both productions were successful and helped give a distinct flavour of recordings made as far as back as the 1940s. The work of cleaning, enhancing and bringing out the original true sound was done by Aodán Ó Dubhghaill.[3]

13

O'Connell's and Other Traditional Pubs

It's Sunday night in the hilltop village of Knocknagree, County Cork. Car headlights can be seen beaming through the darkness and approaching from all roads for the big social night of the week. People come for music, dancing and craic.

Sweet notes echo around the streets and fabled fair green and most people are stepping towards a pub on the northern side. It's already packed to the rafters and a midge would be hard put to find a way in the door. The sign outside says: O'Connell's Traditional Bar. It is one of the most famous of its kind in the country.

Dan O'Connell claims that the national set dancing craze started there in the mid-1960s when sets were not exactly at the top of the popularity charts and it was hard enough to get in customers. But times have changed and everyone, it seems, now wants to dance sets.

O'Connell was born in 1921 in Tureen, a townland outside Knocknagree, and grew up in a typical Sliabh

Luachra environment when most entertainment took place in the home and the ability to dance a set was an asset. He became an excellent athlete and champion cyclist and went farming for a while before he purchased Herlihy's pub, Knocknagree, in 1957. He married Hannah Mary Lucey the following year and they went on to rear their seven children in the premises which was also their family home.

It was a small pub initially, one of fourteen in the village at the time. That seems an enormous number of pubs for a small place, but regular cattle fairs made it easy to obtain intoxicating liquor licences and ensured a certain amount of business for them all. The pub helped to supplement the O'Connell family's income; Dan's main occupation was as a salesman for milking machines and agricultural equipment.

In the early sixties Dan and his friend, Mick Moynihan, used to visit Cahill's bar, Rathmore, for a few sets to the music of Denis Murphy and Johnny O'Leary. The notion struck him that he too could have sets in his Knocknagree premises if he built an extension at the back of the bar, which he did. Set dancing started in O'Connell's on St Stephen's Night 1965, with Denis and Johnny, and it has continued ever since. The original extension has been added on to. It is now the size of an old-style Sliabh Luachra dance hall and the venue for sets on Friday and Sunday nights.

People from many lands visit O'Connell's and one of the countless stories about the place concerns a musician who left Toronto to go to a fleadh cheoil in San Francisco and who by some bizarre quirk of fate ended up in Knocknagree.

The place is a shrine to the renowned Denis Murphy, who died suddenly in 1974 having returned home from a Sunday night session in O'Connell's. Framed pictures of Murphy and friends hang from the walls and there too you will see images of other Sliabh Luachra icons such as Pádraig O'Keeffe and Johnny O'Leary.

Centrepiece of the front bar is a blazing open fire around which people sit whilst listening to sessions or playing card games. It's a dark, old-fashioned pub, panelled with brown wood and with large joists across the ceiling. It's in the more spacious back bar that the dancing takes place and here again the walls are plastered with memorabilia, posters, press clippings, verses of poetry and even more photographs. When feet start tapping to the music, you can feel the spirit and hear the heartbeat of Sliabh Luachra in this place . . . enough to loosen the legs of the tone-deaf.

People from all over the world come to O'Connell's just to see the fun or to learn set dancing. However, it is essentially a place for Sliabh Luachra folk themselves and, despite the pub's attaction for outsiders, O'Connell himself is not prepared to compromise for anybody. He has never charged for admission, explaining: 'If you commercialise the music and put on a cover charge you're allowing customers to dictate the type of entertainment they want. I've always insisted that Irish music and dance should be performed in their truest state, but if people paid they might seek changes to suit their own particular tastes.'

Some leading tourism consultants have suggested that the music has big possibilities for drawing in large numbers of people. But the thought of hordes of visitors disembarking from coaches outside pubs in the area has set alarm bells ringing. The fear is that they might be looking for Irish ballads rendered in a Nashville accent; or if they heard a slow air or a *sean-nós* song, they might think somebody was dead in the house. They mightn't understand, O'Connell cautions.

> We must be very careful about preserving a culture and a tradition that have been handed on from father to son for hundreds of years. We're willing to share our music in Sliabh Luachra, but we don't want it compromised in any way. As I see it, the people, the music and the dancing are the culture and all three are crucial.

You don't have to be an expert dancer to have fun in O'Connell's, as he works on the basis that enjoyment should not be sacrificed for perfection. Denis Murphy, he stresses, loved to see people enjoying themselves and Denis played his music in a way that they would dance to it.

O'Connell enthusiastically led the dancing himself for years and taught many people their first steps. One night in his kitchen he showed me how anyone with a reasonable step could learn in a matter of minutes: he demonstrated some deft footwork even though he had just come out of hospital after surgery. The idea in O'Connell's is to get people on the dance floor. 'The Japanese are lovely dancers and we had no trouble at all in teaching them sets, but the most difficult pupil we ever had was a fellow from inside the Arctic Circle,' he says, with a glint in his eye, getting the international dimension across.

There are no age barriers: young and old all dance together, again underlining the tradition. Some people dance into ripe old age. The late Dan O'Keeffe, of Newquarter, said that dancing sets every weekend in O'Connell's was his secret for remaining hale and hearty. 'Going out and meeting people, the dancing and the music keeps me young at heart,' he said after turning ninety.

The bar is now run by Dan O'Connell's daughter, Mairéad, and her husband, Tim Kiely, a guitar player who accompanies Johnny O'Leary.

JIMMY O'BRIEN'S, KILLARNEY

Painted in the hallowed green and gold of Kerry, a famous pub at Fair Hill, Killarney, catches the eye on the right hand side of the street as one drives into town from Sliabh Luachra. Jimmy O'Brien's has been a magnet for musicians for almost forty years – a meeting place for those coming to the area and a favourite rendezvous of local musicians.

The lively colours reflect the owner's near-fanatical devotion to Kerry football, which is matched only by his interest in traditional music, song and dance. The walls inside are decked with photographs of all the renowned musicians who played there, whilst an old set of uilleann pipes and a concertina from yesteryear are special treasures not to be touched. There's a corner reserved for pictures of All-Ireland winning Kerry teams and some of the county's legendary footballers.

It's a modest hostelry, small by today's standards, but it stands out in a bustling tourist town where trad is a minority taste. 'The majority of tourists don't understand traditional music: it's too complicated for them. I mean it's not easy to sell it to visitors because it's music you can't really hype up. You can't take a traditional air, for instance, and turn it into an old-time waltz,' Jimmy says.

The difficulty with many tourists, he adds, is that they have a very broad view of Irish music. They don't draw a distinction between maudlin Irish-American stuff like 'How Can You Buy Killarney?' and reels played by virtuoso fiddle players, for example.

Like Dan O'Connell he does not believe that the purity of traditional music should be diluted or amended to suit tourists. Also like O'Connell, he has never put on a cover charge for music sessions.

O'Brien grew up in a musical atmosphere at Lyreatough, about six miles east of Killarney, and is rooted in the Sliabh Luachra tradition. He served his time as a motor mechanic in Culloty's garage, Killarney, in the early 1950s before following the emigrant trail to America.

He spent five years in New York, working as a mechanic in the docks, but always wanted to return home even if he had no definite plans for the future. In 1959, he spotted an advertisement in the *Kerryman* newspaper offering for sale a small bar in Killarney owned by Conno Healy. The premises also included a little grocery shop, as was the case with many pubs in those days, and O'Brien and his wife-to-be, Mary Cronin, from Cockhill, Kilcummin, Killarney, decided to purchase the property. The price was £2,700.

Killarney builder Thady O'Neill was given the contract for refurbishing the premises and O'Brien and Mary returned home in 1961, sailing into Cobh on the SS *Sylvania*, a week after getting married.

Ncither had any experience of working in the licensed trade, but were fortunate to engage the services of Breda Cronin, who knew the business backwards, and she worked with them for eight years. 'The general opinion was that I would never make a good publican, but I liked meeting people and that was a big help. Mary, however, took took to it very fast and she was tremendous,' Jimmy recalls.

They were well supported by GAA clubs in East Kerry and by musicians and music lovers. A Comhaltas Ceoltóirí Éireann (CCÉ) branch was founded in Killarney in 1961 and O'Brien was elected chairman, a position he held for 21 years.

Having grown up in Sliabh Luachra, he also had close connections with many musicians, especially his neighbours, the Doyles, who were amongst the earliest patrons of the premises. The Doyles and musicians such as Dan O'Leary, Thade Riordan, David Lynch and Dee Mangan played for regular sessions on Sunday nights.

Unlike O'Connell's in Knocknagree, there was never a big emphasis on set dancing in O'Brien's, although the occasional set was tapped out on the tiled floor. Patrons were more inclined to listen to the music and to singers such as Joan Murphy, Jack Patsy Thade Riordan, Paddy Doyle, Jack Flynn, Jim Kelly, Jerry Kelly and others too numerous to mention.

Denis Murphy, his sister, Julia and Johnny O'Leary played there regularly. Musicians coming to see Murphy invariably met him in O'Brien's, as did broadcasters such as Ciarán Mac Mathúna, who became very friendly with O'Brien. Mentions of the bar on Radio Éireann boosted its profile and it quickly became *the* trad pub in Killarney.

Seán Ó Riada was a regular caller, as were other legendary figures such as Willie Clancy from Clare; Johnny McDonagh, the Galway *sean-nós* singer; Joe Burke, also from Galway; Paddy O'Brien from Tipperary; Nioclás Tóibin from Waterford; Dermot O'Brien, footballer and musician; P. J. Hayes and members of the Tulla Céilí Band; Luke Kelly and Ronnie Drew of The Dubliners; the Glackins from Dublin; Dr Ivor Browne, pipes and tin whistle player; the Cronin brothers, whenever they came home on holidays from the US; and Frankie Gavin of Dé Dannan. And that's by no means a complete list.

The globe-wandering Chieftains have been dropping in for years and have performed in easygoing impromptu sessions before O'Brien's customers – free gratis. Dublin musicians still call there and whenever he's in Killarney one of the country's top trade union officials, Des Geraghty, never fails to turn up with his concert flute.

Of abiding interest are the antique musical instruments and the photo-gallery in the bar. The uilleann pipes on the wall date from between 1830 and 1850 and are being kept 'in custody' for a private owner. The concertina was presented by the late Clare-born musician John Kelly of Capel Street, Dublin, and it belonged to his grandmother. Also on the wall are the hurley and sliotar used by Tipperary goalkeeper Peter O'Sullivan in the 1971 All-Ireland hurling final – a gift to O'Brien's son, Jim.

But it's to the collection of photographs that most people are drawn. Centrepiece is a framed picture of the Killarney ministrel James Gandsey and, as well as the legendary Sliabh Luachra musicians, there are lesser-known characters such as the witty blacksmith Dan Corcoran and Dan 'The Creamery' Murphy, who played the accordeon in the old dance halls.

O'Brien himself is a fine traditional singer with a repertoire of well over a hundred songs, some of which have been collected from him by Tom Munnelly of the

Folklore Commission. Though he needs a bit of coaxing at times, O'Brien loves to sing, especially when he knows he has an appreciative audience, and one of his favourite songs is 'The Groves of Cloghereen'. He has long since known that the most effective way to silence the bar is to sing himself, or in harmony with his daughter, Siobhán.

Sadly, his wife Mary has died, but the pub is still a family affair for the O'Briens, who always have a genuinely warm welcome for musicians, singers, sportsmen and their followers.

Scully's of Newmarket

At the eastern side of Sliabh Luachra, more than thirty miles from Killarney, Scully's in Newmarket, County Cork, is a pub where musicians gather as if by ritual on Monday nights. It's a relaxed kind of tavern where box-player Timmy O'Connor and friends congregate in a room behind the bar, mainly for their own entertainment. But everyone is welcome, both listeners and musicians.

Nobody seems to know exactly when the Monday night sessions started, but they have been going regularly since about 1970. However, music had been played in Scully's, an old pub currently run by Michael Scully, long before that time.

People like Jackie Daly, Séamus Creagh and Cork stalwart Jimmy Crowley started going there in the late sixties. In those days most traditional pubs had a specified night of the week for sessions and Monday was about the only night that was free. Ever since, it has been the night for Scully's.

Here musicians play for pure enjoyment as nobody is hired or paid, and that is the way they want it to be. Tunes are tried out and exchanged and young musicians get tips from veterans. The late Pete Bradley, a tin whistle player from Ballydesmond, once declared that Scully's was 'more of a school than a session' and there was a deal of truth in his no-nonsense assessment.

The jovial Timmy O'Connor has been there from the beginning and he is still the lynchpin. People like Paudie Scully, American piper Denis Brooks, Marie Forrest and Tim Browne are also well-established regulars, as is Raymond O'Sullivan. Musicians from surrounding areas, such as Con Curtin from Brosna, and others from places like Charleville, Newcastlewest and Tournafulla may turn up, and you could also bump into musicians from France, Germany or Sweden.

Anyone can walk in and play in a session. As there's no stage it's a case of pulling up a chair and sitting down with whoever happens to be there at any given time. There could be anything from fifteen to twenty players on a night, or just a handful. In the best spirit of sessions, it just happens on the night – a place where they play rather than perform.

Fiddler Raymond O'Sullivan, who's immersed in the history and lore of the area, describes Scully's as a 'halfway house between the past and the future', pointing out that it's still an integral part of the life of the area. He sees it as a successor to the house-dance era and a refuge for musicians trying to find a new niche in a changed world. There's very little space for dancing, but the floor is cleared the odd night for a set. Songs and recitations are welcome and seanchaí Jim Barry has been known to tell the odd story for appreciative audiences.

For people who like their music in an authentic setting, Scully's is an ideal venue and is a haunt of Americans and people home on holidays from various places in summertime. There's no amplification and you can always have a quiet chat against a musical background.

Newmarket is an earthy town with a good farming hinterland. The area has a strong folk tradition and some of the older musicians and music teachers are still talked about. Jim O'Keeffe, of Ballinahulla, Ballydesmond, who worked with farmers around Kanturk, influenced a number of present-day musicians and men like Deed Connie Murphy and Dan Roger O'Sullivan, who taught music despite being deaf, are names that are often mentioned when tunes are discussed at sessions.

In addition to O'Connell's, O'Brien's and Scully's, sessions are also held in several other pubs in the area.

14

The Masters' Pupils

It would be impossible to count the number of people who learnt from the music masters. You could say hundreds, or even a thousand or two, and nobody could argue with you. The majority of pupils never became well known musicians: they were happy to play in their own homes for their own pleasure and for their own friends.

For that reason anyone trying to list even all of the prominent musicians of the area has an invidious task; it is something that I am certainly not trying to do. This chapter is intended to give a glimpse of some of the talented musicians to emerge in Sliabh Luachra in relatively recent times and if someone's name is not mentioned it doesn't mean that he, or she, is in any way disregarded.

The late Jerry McCarthy, of Scartaglen is a typical example of the innumerable graduates of the Pádraig O'Keeffe academy. Born in 1927, he was the youngest in a family of six and took his first fiddle lesson from O'Keeffe when he was only eight years of age. Jerry's father played concertina and his mother also loved music. Five aunts from the mother's side played concertina as well and there was always music in the house. O'Keeffe was a regular caller and he would sit at the kitchen table whilst methodically writing out tunes. Jerry was a good pupil and was soon able to play at parties in the locality. He won an Oireachtas gold medal in 1947 and always said that slow airs were his forte.

In the late 1950s he travelled to a fleadh cheoil in Thurles with O'Keeffe and Denis Murphy. Unable to find overnight accommodation, the trio had a few hours' sleep in a Morris Minor owned by Denis, which Pádraig christened Murphy's hotel.

Having worked in insurance for several years, he emigrated to New York in 1959. There he met another Kerryman, Bill Fuller, who owned pubs and dance halls and gave the newly-arrived emigrant plenty of work playing music at night. His day job was in a museum where he worked with fellow musician Denis Murphy. The work was light compared to what they had to do back home and they had plenty of craic. In the museum was a statue of the assassinated US President Lincoln. Denis had to take a lift up several floors to dust down the statue and used to quip to Jerry: 'Whoever shot Lincoln gave me a lot of trouble.'

In New York Jerry played with many other Irish musicians, including Joe Burke and Paddy Noonan, and also performed on five occasions in Carnegie Hall, which he found to be quite a nerve-racking experience:

it would have been much more relaxing to be tuning his fiddle in Tom Fleming's bar in Scart.

A gentle, quiet-spoken man with the long, sensitive fingers of a musician, Jerry reckoned that he had between 900 and 1,000 tunes and felt that O'Keeffe had up to 2,000 tunes, a goodly number of which died with him. Jerry returned permanently to Ireland in 1979, settling in Dublin. He lived in the north city suburb of Coolock and was a neighbour of the seanchaí, Éamon Kelly. One of the private joys of Jerry's life was to go upstairs at home, draw the blinds, close the door of his bedroom and play away to his heart's content.

Paddy Cronin, a pupil of O'Keeffe's who is still playing lovely music, emigrated to the US where he spent forty years, mainly in Boston. He hails from a musical Gneeveguilla family and his late brother, Johnny, who also went to America, was a distinguished musician as well. Paddy and his wife Connie now have a home in Killarney.

Paddy sailed to the US in 1949 for, like thousands of others, he had little prospects in Ireland at the time. 'It was all bullwork in Ireland then, a kind of slavery. You'd kill yourself for a £5 note,' remembers Paddy, who cut turf, saved hay and worked in Barna Bog for a while.

In America, Paddy played with musicians from many other parts of Ireland and, influenced by them, has developed a style which is very much his own. Those who know their music put him in the top league and say he has few equals as a reel player. He has made several recordings with O'Byrne de Witt and is well known in Irish music circles across America.

Nowadays, he takes part in pub sessions in Killarney and other places, but stoutly believes that a house is the best place in which to play the fiddle. Pubs are second best, he adds, remarking that there's nothing nicer than sitting down with a crowd by a fire in a house and playing away. He loves to play for himself and also composes tunes.

A pupil of O'Keeffe's who stayed at home is Mikey Duggan from Scartaglen. Both his father and mother played concertina and another key influence was a neighbour, Eileen Spillane, a concertina and fiddle player. He still remembers getting £2 from his mother to purchase his first fiddle in Paddy Nolan's (now Tom Fleming's), Scartaglen.[1]

Mikey continues to play at sessions, but the world has changed a lot since he first played in public at a feis in Scart around 1945. Engagements at stations and house weddings followed and he was soon playing with Pádraig O'Keeffe, Denis Murphy, Johnny O'Leary, the Desmond Céilí Band and other notables.

Genial Mikey loves to tell the story of the night he was cycling home with Denis from a dance. Their fiddles were on the carriers and nearing the Quarry Cross, the light went out on Denis's bike: he hit a big stone and fell off. 'Thank God, 'twas myself that fell and not the fiddle,' declared a relieved Denis as he picked himself up.

Though a non-drinker, Mikey enjoys playing in pubs which he feels are the closest you'll get to the house dances of other days.

Andrew (Sonny) Riordan, of Gneeveguilla, who was born in 1918 and still plays the fiddle, is one of the oldest surviving pupils of O'Keeffe. Andrew says that an amazing thing about the master was that he could converse and write out a tune at the same time. Andrew still has some of the tunes, even though they date to the 1920s, and they are penned in O'Keeffe's impeccable handwriting.

He has a clear recollection of O'Keeffe's first visit to the Riordan family home in Ballinahulla. Having explained the design of the fiddle, the master then showed the new pupil how to hold the fiddle and bow properly and wrote out two easy tunes for him to learn before the next visit.

One could go back to the early days of other surviving old musicians, such as Maurice O'Keeffe and Denis O'Keeffe, to mention just two, and all the time the same stories keeping cropping up.

Nowadays, classes are held on a regular, organised basis in schools and village halls and pupils are given every opportunity to learn music in a formal way. And it's no notice to see several youngsters taking part in music sessions with older musicians from whom they also learn.

At sessions today, the likes of Paudie Gleeson, Jimmy Doyle, Dan Herlihy, John Brosnan, Frank Brosnan (spoons), Johnny Reidy, Denis McMahon and Connie O'Connell can be joined by Paudie and Noeleen O'Connor, Matt Cranitch and his colleagues from the Sliabh Notes group, and others from outside the Sliabh Luachra area. Though eschewed by some purists, the guitar is often played at traditional sessions with guitarists like Tim Gleeson from Gneeveguilla, and Tim Kiely from Knocknagree, falling in with fiddlers and box-players.

Paudie Gleeson of Gneeveguilla is from the Pádraig O'Keeffe school of music, to which he was introduced by his friend the late Johnny Cronin. Paudie got his first fiddle in Mikey Murphy's of Dereen, and he still remembers Johnny playing for him in Tureenamult bog as they returned home from Mikey's on a Sunday evening. All of Paudie's eight children play music and are well able to make a session purr.

Nicky McAuliffe and Pádraig Moynihan are musicians as well as music teachers, ensuring that the tradition is carried on. One of those keeping the fiddle tradition alive is a young Gneeveguilla man Connie Moynihan. But there is concern for the future of fiddle playing in the area and the instrument, which has always been so closely identified with Sliabh Luachra music, is not nearly as popular as it was formerly.

Many, many people are playing music nevertheless and the above-named are just a sample of all those who are involved in one way or another.

One of the most talented musicians to emerge in

recent times is twenty-year-old Emma O'Leary of Scartaglen, who won three gold medals at the 1999 All-Ireland Fleadh Cheoil in Wexford. Emma was awarded first prize in competitions on the tin whistle, slow airs on the tin whistle, and slow airs on the fiddle. She is taking a folk theatre studies course at the Insitute of Technology in Tralee, and also teaches music.

Very much involved in the contemporary scene is the husband-and-wife team, Liam and Lisa O'Connor, who present their own productions in what could be described as modern trad style. Accordeonist Liam is from Newmarket and Lisa is from Boherbue. Liam has travelled all over the world with the Michael Flatley *Lord of the Dance* show. The couple continue to develop international audiences.

Part II

Music in Words

15

Music in Words

Making words dance is another long-cherished custom in Sliabh Luachra.

Everyone knows about the cheery notes that come from pipes and strings, but poets make music with words: the arts are intertwined and there are remarkable similarities between the bohemian lives of poets and musicians, larger than life people such as Eoghan Rua Ó Súilleabháin and Pádraig O'Keeffe being typical examples. Both started out as teachers, but were forced to forsake the classroom for the lifestyle of a roving poet and musician, respectively.

As well as Aodhagán Ó Rathaille and Ó Súilleabháin, the area has a host of poets who span the centuries and some are achieving distinction today. Who would ever think that a man who was born and brought up near Cullen, County Cork, would win the prestigious Whitbread prize for a collection of poems which draws from his experiences in his native place? That's what Bernard O'Donoghue did in 1993–94.

There was hardly a townland in Sliabh Luachra

which in times past didn't have a wordsmith to record events in verse which mightn't mean much to the wider world but which were important to the local people. Nearly always male, they were not only poets but elders of a sort, who wrote letters on behalf of people, helped draft wills, arbitrated in disputes between neighbours about land, gave sound advice on myriad matters and even made matches between eligible young men and women.

They were respected – sometimes feared – for their literary abilities. They could eulogise a person, but they had an equal facility to destroy a reputation with a few, well chosen acerbic words. Some of the verse could be described as doggerel poetry, but it still conveys a word-picture of another sort of world and reflects attitudes of particular times. Many of the poets didn't have much education, but in the days before Donagh O'Malley's yellow buses started taking students to schools in the area, they were looked up to by a people who didn't have a great deal of formal education themselves.

Poems were learnt by heart by illiterate people, and were often recited at social gatherings or around cottage firesides on winter nights. And just like the musical tradition, the poems were handed on from one generation to the next. We have a graphic image from the 1940s of the late Charlie O'Leary, of Gullane, Gneeveguilla, reading aloud a song by Aodhagán Ó Rathaille. In a poem by Tadhg Ua Duinnín we can see Charlie with his feet planted in a rushy field while herding his cows, his voice booming and droning as if monks were intoning, a solitary figure lost in poetry. Ua Duinnín says the scholarly Charlie was the rightful heir to the long line of hedge schoolmasters.[1]

In the public mind, certain privileges were allowed to poets. Some were known to possess odd traits, but people expected them to have eccentricities that wouldn't be common in 'normal' folk.

The area has always had a high regard for learning and scholarship – something people like to think has been inherited from the old bardic schools and courts of poetry. According to tradition, one or more bardic schools flourished in the area, followed later by a court of poetry where the study of Irish verse was the main business. Poor scholars travelled there on foot from places where such gatherings ceased to exist and some of these students afterwards entered European universities to become priests. Others joined the armies of France, Austria or Spain.

The old big houses where lived the native Irish ruling families until their overthrow in the 17th century were repositories of poetry and patrons of poets such as Aodhagán Ó Rathaille. It ought not to be forgotten that there is also a very practical reason for the store set on learning in Sliabh Luachra: the opportunity education offers of improving one's lot economically and financially – a priority consideration.

Some poets, such as Dónall Ó Conchubhair, of Cullen, who died in 1930, wrote in Irish; a book of his poems was published after his death. Two other local poets in living memory were Joe Dinneen of Rathmore, and Ned Buckley of Knocknagree, both deceased, and many of their verses have been published in newspapers and historical journals over the years.[2]

Professor Daniel Corkery, author of *The Hidden Ireland*, wrote that Sliabh Luachra was once the literary capital of Ireland and he further observed:

> Milk and honey may, indeed, have actually been the most plentiful of foods in it and if it were so it was only fitting for nowhere else in Ireland were so many sweet singers gathered together. The south-west corner of Munster was the Attica of Irish Ireland and Sliabh Luachra its Hymetus.

16

Aodhagán Ó Rathaille (*c.* 1670–1726)

Glancing at lichen-covered stones on a roadside ditch in the heart of Sliabh Luachra today it's hard to realise that in this humble spot stood the home of the great Gaelic poet Aodhagán Ó Rathaille, known to scholars as the Dante of Munster.

His traditional birthplace at Scrahanaville, in what is now a farmer's haggard two miles west of Gneeveguilla, is marked by a simple limestone slab, shaded by palm, sycamore and rhododendron trees. As the breeze whistles through the leaves in this peaceful place the imagination wanders back over the centuries to the turbulent era in which the poet lived.

Though much of his verse lives on, little enough is known of Ó Rathaille, except that he moved around west Munster, never going further than Cork city, and that he was a poet of the landed and the wealthy rather than of the poor, although the poor formed the overwhelming majority of the population in those days. Much of his work bemoans the fall of the big houses and the degradation that followed the victories of Cromwell, the Battle of the Boyne and the Treaty of Limerick.

Indeed he comes across as a pessimistic figure lamenting the fall of the rich and mighty, of himself and of Ireland. But that impression should not be allowed to diminish his high standing as one of the most critically regarded Gaelic poets.

Unlike his colourful successor, Eoghan Rua Ó Súilleabháin, there is not much of an oral tradition surrounding Ó Rathaille. One of the surviving anecdotes shows the human, even witty, side of him. It tells of a day he went into a bookshop in Cork, roughly dressed and looking every inch of a country *cábóg* [yokel]. He took up a large book in Greek or Latin and asked what price it was. Cleverly enough he was looking at it upside down and the shopkeeper, sizing up a strange character, told him he could have it for nothing if he could read it. Of course he proved straight away that he could and the shopkeeper was made to honour the commitment.

During Ó Rathaille's lifetime, Gaelic and Catholic Ireland was suppressed. The Gaelic majority had no military powers, no army, no civil, or religious, rights, and everything possible was being done to kill the soul of the people.

> It was left to the poet and songwriter to breathe the ancient spirit of the Gael of Ireland into that nondescript mass; to charm their hearts with his

> melody. He seemed to feel instinctively that if time could only be gained, if the people could be charmed by his melody and song . . . the cloud of oppression would lift in time and would reveal a people marvellously united . . . [1]

Ó Rathaille came from comfortable stock who left County Cavan after the confiscation of their lands in 1653. His father, John Ó Raghaillaigh (O'Reilly – which became O'Rahilly in Sliabh Luachra), was also a Gaelic poet, and Aodhagán's mother was a Miss Egan O'Reilly. According to local lore, she owned much of the townland of Scrahanaville.

Aodhagán's father had studied in the bardic schools, some of which still survived into his own time, and it was in them also that the young poet was educated, picking up a knowledge of the classics and genealogy, in particular. Life in Ireland was changing substantially for the worse as he grew up and adult conversation must surely have featured the hanging of another famous Kerry poet, Piaras Feiritéar, at Martyrs' Hill, Killarney. The O'Rahilly family was also evicted from their lands at Scrahanaville. Aodhagán gives full vent to the grief he feels at the laying waste of the land, the levelling of forests, the plundering of the country and the downfall of his rich patrons, the Gaelic nobility.

Ó Rathaille's poetry can be broadly divided into three categories – elegies, satires and shorter lyrics. Twelve of his elegies survive and they are a sort of final tribute to the Gaelic gentry. Much of his poetry survived for generations in the mouths of an illiterate peasantry who learned the elegies, some of which are very long, by heart. These elegies sing the praises of their subjects, trace their pedigree, tell how nature itself mourns them and how their passing would forever be regretted.

An example is this English version of a verse from his elegy on Dómhnall Ó Ceallacháin[2]:

Son of Ceallachan, the manly, the high-spirited, the vivacious,
Son of Conchubhar, a noble who was bold and brave,
Son of Donogh, son of Tadhg, the staying strength of the learned,
Son of Conchubhar Laighneach, who did not show weakness.

Ó Rathaille glorifies the lavish lifestyle and hospitality of the richer classes whose patronage he enjoyed, which was in sharp contrast to the plight of the ordinary people, most of whom struggled to eke out an existence. The wealth and hospitality of the Gaelic nobility are evoked by another verse in the Ó Ceallacháin elegy:

Dóirse gan dúnadh ar dhúntaibh ómrach,
Céir dá lasadh ar gach balla agus seomra,
Caise dá mbriseadh dhon bhfuirinn gach nóimeat,
'S gan trághadh lachta ag teacht san ól soin.

[The doors wide open on enclosures bright as amber,
Warlights blazing from every wall and chamber,
Every moment fresh casks open for the multitude
With no ebb in the liquid coming to that drinking feast.[

The poet was also a dab hand at tracing relations and in a long-winded way he follows the lineage of Ó Ceallacháin back to Enos, son of Seth, son of Adam, who started all the trouble.

Ó Rathaille gives not only a local but a national insight into Gaelic civilisation and the way life was lived in those days of the 17th and early 18th centuries.

> The attitude of mind in them (the elegies) is as valuable as the pictures they give us of the big house, of the hunting, the gambling, the watchman in the cattle field at night, the dependence of the swarming poor on the few rich that controlled the countryside. Not only are they a surer guide to the history of the place and period than the official statements, but they are a swifter guide while, at the same time, they bring us deeper into the heart of things.[3]

His satires are not regarded by most critics as remarkable and reflect the style of Irish literature of the era, but he certainly proved that he could dip his quill in vitriol and destroy his enemies with a few biting words, such as those he wrote about a fellow poet, Domhnall na

Tuile, who had written in unflattering terms of himself:

> *Soraire, sramach, sopaire salach,*
> *Rothaire, reatha an breagaire;*
> *Crotaire tana, slogaire smeartha,*
> *Sliogeas gach treas 'n a chraosgoile.*

The English translation could never convey the full power and venom of the lines:

> *A fellow full of vermin, of running eyes, a dirty gaunt wad,*
> *A fugitive vagabond is the liar,*
> *A slender hunchback, a greasy swallower,*
> *Who swallows every rubbish into his greedy maw.*

Ó Rathaille is best remembered for his lyrics, which had as themes a broken Ireland and himself as an equally broken poet.

Professor Daniel Corkery, who closely studied the poets of Munster, their life and times, rhapsodises about Ó Rathaille's lyrics in *The Hidden Ireland,* a seminal study of Gaelic Munster and its literary figures in the 18th century.

> A lyric is happy in as much as it sings, sings spontaneously, swiftly, sweetly, brilliantly. So tried, his lyrics are true and sterling. The poets of that century were, it seems to me, the first adequately

to respond to the music that had been ripening in the language for hundreds of years.[5]

Ó Rathaille's most famous lyric, 'Gile na Gile' ('Brightest of the Bright'), is one of the first aisling poems ever written and has been compared to the first movement of a Mozart sonata, full of rhythm and melody and flawlessly constructed. The first verse runs:

Gile na gile do chonnarc are slighe na n-uaigneas;
Criostal an chriostail a guirmruisc rinn-uaine;
Binneas an bhinnis a friotal nár chríon-ghruamdha;
Deirge is finne do fionnadh n-a gríos-ghruadhnaibh

Again, an English translation does scant justice to this classic lyric:

The Brightest of the Bright met me on my path so lonely;
The Crystal of all Crystals was her flashing dark-blue eye;
Melodious more than music was her spoken language only;
And glorious were her cheeks of a brilliant crimson dye.

Ó Rathaille ended his troubled life in poverty and said farewell to the world with the following lines, which may have been the last he ever wrote:

Stadfad-sa, is gar dam éag gan maill,
Ó treascradh dreagain Leamhan, Léin, is Laoi;
Rachad-sa a haithle searc na laoch don chill,
Na flatha fá raibh mo shean roimh éag do Chríost.

[I will cease now, death is nigh unto me without delay;
Since the warriors of the Laune, of Lein, and of the Lee have been laid low,
I will follow the beloved among heroes to the grave,
Those princes under whom were my ancestors before the death of Christ.]

Judging from the mood of his poems, death could hardly have come soon enough to this remarkable poet, whose mortal remains now lie in Muckross Abbey, Killarney.

17

The Charismatic Eoghan Rua Ó Súilleabháin (1748–84)

If all the stories are true, the poet Eoghan Rua Ó Súilleabháin was undoubtedly one of Sliabh Luachra's most flamboyant and tragic characters. His work and personality have been compared with those of the Scottish poet, Robbie Burns. More than two hundred years after his death, Ó Súilleabháin lives on in the folk memory with tales of his exploits being passed on to succeeding generations.

He is, however, more popularly remembered as a rake and womaniser than as a poet: his image is of a handsome man holding court in a shebeen, or being hunted out of one place or another by some indignant priest following 'indiscretions' with young ladies. He never married but is reputed to have had many offspring.

Unlike Robbie Burns, whose life has been well chronicled, we don't know that much about Ó Súilleabháin. His life has almost certainly been over-romanticised and the stories about him have been embellished in all the tellings. Legends aside, he seems to have had a hard life and he died a miserable death in a fever hut in Knocknagree, aged only thirty-six, without realising his full potential as a poet.

We also know that he received a good education, that he was bilingual and that, as well as being a poet, he was a teacher, soldier, and *spailpín* (travelling farm labourer). He had a restless personality, and the picture we have is of a wild character who was the centre of attention in taverns where his songs were sung and where music and dance formed an essential part of the scene.

Whatever about his reputation as a rake, he is one of the main reasons for the literary renown of Sliabh Luachra. Unlike the more accomplished Ó Rathaille, Ó Súilleabháin was more of a 'people's poet' and ordinary folk could get better value from his verses.

Essayist and critic Con Houlihan, whilst granting that *Eoghan an Bhéil Bhinn* (Eoghan of the sweet mouth) was a good scholar and a brilliant technician, claims that much of his verse was no more than a kind of verbal music.

> You will search in vain if you wish to find the world of his time and place expressed. There are fragments of reality – but no more. And it is hardly surprising – for him poetry was a vehicle in which to seek temporary escape from a life of toil and penury . . . And no doubt he was in-

> fluenced by what his public – such as it was – wanted. The people of Sliabh Luachra hardly longed to hear about the kind of life they knew too well – they didn't see poetry in cutting turf or digging spuds or picking stones.[1]

Eoghan was descended from the O'Sullivans of Cappanacushy Castle, Kenmare, who came to the Sliabh Luachra area around the time of Cromwell, having been driven out of their native place. Eoghan's father, Parthalán, had quite a considerable holding in the townland of Meentogues, over two miles south-west of Gneeveguilla village, and the family would have been far better off than most others in the area.

Eoghan attended the nearby school (all traces of which have vanished) at Faha, nowadays known as Annaghmore. According to an t-Athair Pádraig Ua Duinnín[2], Faha also housed a classical academy where Irish, English, Latin and Greek were taught. A court of poetry used also be held there, with scholars and poets from counties Cork and Limerick attending.

One of the best regarded authorities on Eoghan Rua is an t-Athair Ua Duinnín, who was reared in the area and who devoted a good deal of his life to collecting and studying the works of the Sliabh Luachra poets. Ua Duinnín was born in 1860 and his closeness to Eoghan's own time enhances his standing as an authority on the poet.

The priest scholar, who grew up listening to Eoghan's

poems and songs in his own home, describes Eoghan Rua as follows: 'He was five feet eight or nine inches in height. He stood erect and his face was of a distinctly handsome cast. He dressed in the costume of the time, a swallow-tail frieze coat and breeches reaching to the knee.'

Professor Daniel Corkery says that Eoghan was good-looking, with hair as golden as red, not indeed far different from the colour of his sun-tanned brow and cheeks; narrow-headed, high-crowned, lithe, tall, swirling, carrying himself well, daring and not easily put down; full of life, witty and given to laughing. Yet he could be very still over a book and very patient in copying a manuscript.[3]

When he was eighteen Eoghan opened a school in Gneeveguilla. It didn't last long for, after a young lady in the locality presented him with his child, he had to flee. In a similar vein, the folk tradition has it that while he was acting as a teacher in Knocknagree, the parish priest, Fr Ned Fitzgerald, found him one day with a young lady in a hayshed near the school. When asked by the priest what he was doing, the quick-witted poet is reported to have replied, 'I'm teaching this girl English grammar. She can parse, but cannot decline.'[4]

Earlier, the poet had put in verse his message to Fr Fitzgerald that he planned to start a school in Knocknagree:

Reverend Sir –
Please to publish from the altar of your holy Mass
That I will open school at Knocknagree Cross
Where the tender babes will be well off,
For it's there I'll teach them their criss-cross . . .

Not being suited to the discipline of the schoolroom, he took to the roads as a spailpín with a spade on his shoulder, joining hordes of other young men who earned their bread the hard way, picking potatoes and doing other farming tasks.

Given Eoghan's wit, roguery and likeability, it's hard to envisage him slaving in the fields for too long and he was the type of individual who had the ability to get around the toughest of masters. Whenever the opportunity arose, he went back to teaching and had schools in parts of County Cork. He also attended courts of poetry in different areas.

There are plenty of examples to prove Eoghan's gift of wordplay in Irish, or English. There is evidence of how articulate he was in English in the following excerpt from an advertisement which he wrote for a farmer selling a horse – a verbal agility that would put many of today's trendy copywriters to shame:

A sorel steed of superlative symmetry, styled Spanker, and a snip square-sided, slender-shouldered, smart-sighted, with a small star, and steps singularly stately; free from strain, spasms, stringhalt, stranguary, sciatica, staggers, scaling, sollander, surfeit, seams, scouring, strange, strenuous swelling, soreness, scratches, splint, squint . . .

There were numerous twists and turns in his eventful, though short, life. In 1780, another dalliance forced him to leave Ireland and join the British navy. While acting as a tutor to the Nagle family, near Fermoy, County Cork, he is believed to have seduced either a servant girl or a daughter of his employer, and to have had to make a run for it.

Having enlisted, he joined a British fleet which set sail to the West Indies and took part in a battle with the French. The British, under Vice-Admiral Rodney, were victorious. Unhappy in the navy, Eoghan had to come up with a ruse to get out, so what better way than by writing a poem which flattered old Rodney, entitled 'Rodney's Glory':

Twas in the year of Eighty Two,
The Frenchmen knew full well 'tis true
Brave Rodney did their fleet subdue
Not far from old Fort Royal.

In any case, he was back in Sliabh Luachra in 1784 doing what he knew best – writing verse and generally enjoying life.

In the summer of that year, he wrote an ode in praise of Colonel Daniel Cronin of Killarney, who had lately been promoted to be head of a local band of military. Cronin was not impressed with the poem so the angry poet wrote a biting satire which the colonel didn't like one bit. Some of Cronin's henchmen subsequently attacked Eoghan in a Killarney public house and he sustained serious injuries, having been hit over the head with an iron weapon – a tongs, according to local tradition.

His head bandaged and now suffering from a fever, the wayward poet returned to Knocknagree and died penniless in a hut at the eastern end of the village, close to where the church now stands. A plaque erected by Cumann Luachra near the spot is suitably engraved with his last words in the form of a rhyming couplet:

Sin é an file go fann
Nuair a thiteann an peann as a lámh.

[Weak indeed is the poet
When the pen falls from his hand.]

Eoghan's poetry is noted for its intellectualism, sense of form, articulation, freshness of vision and its musical quality. His extant works, collected by an tAthair Ua Duinnín, includes nineteen aislingí, an elegy, satires, poems about his own life and poems in praise of women.

According to Ua Duinnín, he composed poetry in a language which was so much in the spoken language that ordinary people revelled in it.

> He presses into service the conventions of the traditional poets, but only as a means to float his melody and add distinctiveness to the outlines of his picture. His aislingidhe, or poetical visions, have had a profound influence on the social and political outlook of the people. They found their way into the dwellings of rich and poor . . . to our fathers and grandfathers and to some of those of us who have passed into middle age, the Eoghan Rua tradition has been vivid and inspiring. His name is a household word not only in Kerry, but throughout the greater part of Munster.[5]

Ua Duinnín goes on to extol the glories of Eoghan's poetry, saying that perhaps there was never a poet so entirely popular; that his songs were sung everywhere and that Munster was spellbound for generations.

Eoghan's songs were sung by the peasantry and of special appeal were those that concerned his rakish life as a spailpín, which he regrets in one of his works as follows:

> *Is searbh an aiste liom labhairt ar cheithlinn,*
> *Tigh an tabhairne seanaim mar chaitheas mo stór,*
> *Dearbhaim, admhuighim feasta, 'gus géillim*
> *Gur damanta an chéird i, is to mb'fhearr leigeann dóibh.*

[Bitter it is to me to speak of a woman,
I shun the tavern where I spent my all,
I swear, I admit henceforth, I yield
That it is a damned business and they are better let alone.]

Ua Duinnín and others have eulogised Eoghan, even describing him as the Robbie Burns of Ireland, pointing to the similarities in character between the two poets – the same unstable, highly strung temperament and love of socialising, women and humanity in general – not to speak of the clerical disfavour they both attracted.

Latter-day critics do not agree completely with the fulsome tributes paid to Eoghan Rua by an t-Athair Ua Duinnín and others. One such critic, Tadhg Ua Duinnín, says that Eoghan composed mediocre, fair, good and very good poems and songs: 'Sometimes his seeming preoccupation with trivia tended to take from his stature as a poet. But, on the other hand, these exercises and his almost impudent challenges to those who regarded themselves as his betters, and his disregard for the norms of society, may well indeed have enhanced his reputation.'[6]

Technically, he says, Eoghan Rua was a poet of no mean calibre, a weaver of words, a master of assonance, and even though he used the simpler forms of metre to a great extent, he had a knowledge of the more intricate metrical arrangements.

Given the kind of life Eoghan led, it comes as no

surprise that controversy still surrounds the location of his last resting place. On the day his remains were removed from Knocknagree for burial in Muckross Abbey, Killarney, the heavens opened, with the result that the cortège was unable to cross the flooded River Blackwater. Local tradition has it that the body was temporarily interred at Nohoval cemetery, close to the Knocknagree side of the Blackwater.

It is generally believed that he was eventually buried in Muckross Abbey, but this view is by no means unanimously accepted. Well-known local historian and folklorist Dan Cronin insists that 'contrary to what has been said and despite what has been written, a strong and genuine tradition in this area tells us that Eoghan Rua sleeps his last long sleep in an unmarked grave in Nohoval cemetery.'[7]

The clear outline of the remains of a cabin where Eoghan Rua lived can still be seen in a field in Meentogues, which has a limestone plaque near the entrance gate.

18

Fr Dinneen: the Dictionary Man

One of the most brilliant scholars to emerge from Sliabh Luachra in the past two hundred years was, indisputably, Fr Patrick Stephen Dinneen. Because of his utter commitment to the revival of the Irish language, he became known as an tAthair Ua Duinnín and is best remembered for his famous Irish–English dictionary which was first published in 1904, with the larger edition coming in 1927.

But he was much more than a lexicographer. He was also a writer, a poet, a mathematician, a controversialist and a complex, eccentric personality – to say the least. The son of struggling tenant farmers, Matthew and Mary Dinneen, who had about ten hungry acres at Corran, four miles south-west of Rathmore, he was born on Christmas Day 1860. One of ten children, Patrick attended Meentogues national school where his uncle, Michael O'Donoghue (Mick the Master), was teaching. A reserved boy, he was a dedicated pupil and a lover of books and learning – traits in keeping with the traditions of the Dinneen clan. He remained a pupil in Meentogues until he became a monitor whilst in his teens.

Irish was still spoken in the area and was the main language of the Dinneen household. In his youth, Patrick, growing up in the aftermath of the Great Famine, personally experienced hardship and eviction and the family was forced to move house on a few occasions. His father was a sheep dealer who travelled widely to fairs in the south and was a shrewd, intelligent man of the world. Mary Dinneen was a hard-working, deeply religious woman and, according to folk tradition, was regarded by many people as a saint.

Having shown obvious potential as a student, Patrick was tutored in Latin by Fr Cornelius O'Sullivan, Rathmore, and entered the Jesuit (Society of Jesus) Novitiate at Milltown, Dublin, in September 1880. He took an honours BA degree in modern literature and mathematics at the Royal University and was conferred with an honours MA in maths in 1889. He then studied theology at Milltown and was ordained a priest by Archbishop Walsh at the Jesuit Church of St Francis Xavier, Gardiner Street, Dublin, in July 1894. For a few years after he taught at Jesuit colleges including Clongowes and Mungret, often making the journey on foot from Clongowes to Maynooth college where he would copy the work of Kerry poets from manuscripts.

An tAthair Ua Duinnín's first poem and novel were published around the turn of the century and he began collecting the poems of Aodhagán Ó Rathaille at that time. The year 1900 marked a turning point in his life for he left the Jesuit order. The reasons he did so remain unclear. The order has strongly rejected claims that he went his own way because of differences over the dictionary, or a dispute about royalties from his varied literary activities. The more likely reason is that Ua Duinnín, who was strong-headed, a loner and sometimes difficult to get on with, found it hard to accept the discipline of the order. Nor would he be able to give the high level of commitment he desired to the revival of Irish whilst a member of the order.

According to the superior of the order, an tAthair John J. Coyne:

> De réir mar a bhí se ag dul in aois, mhothaigh an tAthair O Duinnín saol an Chumainn rud beag dian air, toisc é bheith aonaorach ón nádúr agus toisc e bheith beagáinín corr ann fein freisin. Thaobhaigh a chuid uachtarán leis an rud a rinne se, óir chonachtas dóibh gurbh fhearr an úsáid a d'fhéadfaí a bhaint as a chuid talanna taobh amuigh d'ord crábhaidh.[1]

> [As he was growing older, Fr Dinneen felt the life of the Society a little difficult because he was detached by nature and also because he was a little unusual in personality. His superiors agreed with what he did because it was clear to them that greater use could be made of his talents outside a religious order.]

As Fr Coyne remarked in that last sentence, an tAthair Ua Duinnín made the best of use of his freedom to develop his talents outside the order. As well as his first dictionary, he produced fifteen books in Irish, gave Irish classes and visited the Gaeltacht early in the century. He became a leading figure with Conradh na Gaeilge in the national revival and was active in that body's publications committee with Pádraig Pearse. He continued to turn out scholarly works and was a prolific contributor to Gaelic magazines, newspapers and periodicals of the day.

This love of the language shines through in his writings as the following extract, published in the period between 1902 and 1904, illustrates:

> The language is the root on which all the other elements are grafted and it is the language in its living state, and not the language as found in books and manuscripts, that is the true basis of this general national revival . . . The national language is the poor man's literature and folklore, it is his history and tradition, it reflects what he knows of his own country and the outer world, it is his fund of music and song . . . I for one, had I to choose, as I hope I never shall have to choose, between the ruins of Tara and the living Irish tongue, would not hesitate to say, perish Tara, but leave me the language of the Gael in its living state.[2]

Other people worked with him on the Irish–English dictionary, among them J. J. O'Kelly (Sceilg), who was a prominent journalist and author in Dublin at the time. and a leading collaborator in the production of the dictionary. A native of Valentia, County Kerry, O'Kelly was Minister for Education in the Republican government of 1921. O'Kelly reported that Ua Duinnín was in poor health at the time, looking gaunt and anaemic and acting very moodily – the weight of the undertaking was taking its toll. But the completion of the dictionary brought much mental relief and, according to O'Kelly, 'there was an instant improvement in his general health which, to our general delight, was maintained until he became quite robust.'[3]

Most of Ua Duinnín's time was spent in the National Library in Dublin and he was also involved in the establishment of Coláiste na Mhumhan, the first training college for teachers of Irish. He had several rows with other members of Conradh na Gaeilge, until finally he left the organisation in 1909, following the controversy over the attitude of some bishops to compulsory Irish in universities.

The scholarly priest has many achievements to his name, including what was regarded as the first novel in Irish, *Cormac Ua Conaill* (1901). From a Sliabh Luachra viewpoint he gets the kudos for focusing attention on the work of the Munster poets, notably Ó Rathaille and Ó Súilleabháin, about whom he would have heard a great deal in his youth when they would still have been very much alive in the folk memory. Stones from Eoghan Rua's house were, according to local tradition, used in the building of the school which the priest had attended as a child in Meentogues.

The priest did invaluable work in collating, editing and publishing collections of poems of the poets from his area. He also went to endless lengths to get his hands on the manuscripts which were then available.

An tAthair Ua Duinnín wrote several school text-books, plays and essays, and a number of poems. Though not generally known as a poet – his talents were channelled in other directions – he could have held his own with the best of them had he devoted more of his time to writing poetry. The following is the first verse of his 'Looking Out For The Spaniards':

Sorrow darkens Desmond's valleys, sorrow muffles Desmond's hills,
Sorrow's voice in plaintive cadence sounds through Desmond's thousand rills;
For the spoiler's hand has cursed her, from the Galtees to the sea,
Where all shattered and dismantled smokes in ruins proud Dunbuidhe.

From the time he left the Jesuits, an tAthair Ua Duinnín's status as a priest was *suspensus a divinis*, which in effect meant that he could not say Mass or administer the sacraments. The Jesuit order stressed, however, that he left with full permission and that later in his life he rejected an offer to allow him celebrate Mass again. For more than thirty years, he was a personality on the streets of Dublin and made friends with people of every station, including the poor. He was also known as a priest who loved children and enjoyed quizzing them and passing on his knowledge of Irish to them. Sceilg recalled how he would visit his home on Sunday afternoons, rarely calling without chocolate for his children, with whom he felt as much at home as their elders. Sceilg said he was excellent company, quite at ease in all circles, sparking with repartee and punning with all the abandon and sprightliness of youth.

Towards the end of his life, he lived in lodgings at Portmarnock, a seaside suburb to the north of Dublin, and took the train each morning to the City centre, with the National Library his usual destination. A distinctive figure, he used to wear an old-style top hat, a long black coat, baggy pants and good strong boots, and carried a bundle of books and papers in his arms.

Whenever he returned to his old home at Corran, he would work in a little room attached to the house (which is no longer there). But he didn't spend all his time in the room and there are people who can still picture in the mind's eye the solitary figure in black walking along the road westwards towards Killarney.

He died on 29 September 1934 in St Vincent's Hospital in Dublin, having collapsed a few days before in the National Library. The last rites were given to him by a Jesuit. Whatever about his split from the Jesuits, an tAthair Ua Duinnín remained a regular churchgoer throughout his life, had conservative views and often defended the position of the Church in public controversies.

His funeral was a noteworthy occasion in Dublin. Solemn requiem Mass was celebrated in the Jesuit church in Gardiner Street, and amongst the huge attendance were Éamon de Valera and Seán T. O'Kelly, both of whom went on to become presidents of Ireland, as well as leading academics and literary personalities of the day.

He was laid to rest in the poets' corner of Glasnevin cemetery.

A monument in Killarney bears testimony to this day to the achievements of Ua Duinnín. He was responsible for getting the statue of a *spéirbhean* erected close to the spot on Martyr's Hill in the town where the west Kerry poet, Piaras Feiritéar, was hanged by Cromwellian forces in 1653. The monument also honours the Glenflesk poet Seafraidh Ó Donnchadha as well as Sliabh Luachra's Aodhagán Ó Rathaille and Eoghan Rua Ó Súilleabháin. Ua Duinnín is also credited with having had erected a plaque commemorating the poets at Muckross Abbey in Killarney.

19

A Shared Love of Poetry and Song

What has an Oxford don specialising in medieval English and the man who wrote the original version of the Australian hit song of the 1950s, 'A Pub with No Beer', got in common? It's not an easy question and a strange pairing they'd make if they met in Dan O'Connell's pub some night.

But Bernard O'Donoghue and Dan Sheahan would have much in common, not least their love of poetry. Bernard, from Knockduff, Cullen, is a winner of the Whitbread prize for poetry, whilst Dan, from Newmarket, penned the song which was recorded by Slim Dusty and reached the number two spot in the British Top Twenty all those years ago.

Both are part of the timeless 'way with words' tradition. Dan has long since flown on to Elysian fields, but Bernard, a Fellow of English at Wadham College, Oxford, is still writing fine poetry. According to his London publishers, Chatto and Windus, O'Donoghue's great skill is to give the impression of recalling memories for the very first time, memories that are inextricably linked to the here and now, as if an experience in early life had been waiting to find its significance in the present day.

After the sudden death of his father in 1962, Bernard's family moved to Manchester. Having studied for a university degree in mediaeval English, he took up a teaching post at Magdalen College, Oxford, but never lost touch with his roots in Cullen, where he now has a holiday home. Music venues such as Dan O'Connell's and Scully's, and townlands such as Glash and Lisrobin feature in his poems.

This poem, 'The City at Shrone', was written by Bernard O'Donoghue in April–May 1999:

A strange place for a city, Shrone, where
The mountain rain drifts along the western Pap
And the fields drain downwards to Rathmore.

Still, it is a strange city. One small house,
Single-chimneyed, whitewashed and tethered to
A disconnected ESB pole near the ramparts.

Half as old as time. The blessed virgin shelters
In her glass grotto, her blue mantle fading
Like the sky, the beads round her neck rusting.

Maybe, after all, it's not such a foolish place
For a city: its long-past citizens sleep well,
Unvisited by showers of high explosive.

The late north-Kerry writer Dr Bryan MacMahon recorded his impression of walking through Oxford one day and chatting with the Cullen man:

> Here, I tell myself, with increasing appreciation, is a brilliant scholar who, though widely immersed in medieval literature and now on the threshold of wide recognition as a poet of rare quality, is still firmly rooted in the clay of Sliabh Luachra. Here is a man equipped by natural aptitude and training to appreciate the true values of both Chaucer and Eoghan Rua Ó Súilleabháin.[1]

O'Donoghue, a friend of Seamus Heaney, the Nobel Prize winning poet, is an unassuming man with a deep attachment to his birthplace:

> I like living in England in many ways. It is lively and thronged and various and it has been generous to me. But there is something about Cullen. I remember very well my first return after moving to England. I remember standing in Jer Mac's gate field at the top of Knockduff, seeing again the houses in Doon looking back at me across the Ceannadas and Islandbrack, and knowing that I would never feel at home anywhere else.

Long before O'Donoghue's time another prominent poet in the locality was Edward Walsh (1805–50). He lived around Doon, between Knocknagree and Boherbue, attended a hedge school and later became a teacher. He is best remembered, however, for his articles and poems and for his translations from Irish to English. He is credited with having translated some of Eoghan Rua's poems, which would have been in wide circulation in Irish in his time.

Walsh himself wrote poetry in English; the opening verse of 'O'Donovan's Daughter' is an example of his style:

One midsummer eve when the Bel-fire was lighted,
And the bagpiper's tune called the maidens delighted,
I joined the gay throng by the Araglen water,
And danced till the dawn with O'Donovan's daughter.[2]

Also in the Cullen area lived Dónall Ó Conchubhair, who wrote in the Irish that was spoken in Duhallow during the 19th century. Despite having little formal education, he was regarded as an excellent poet. The following is a tribute to the bravery of those who fought in the Easter Rising of 1916:

Scéal Luain na Cásca, go deo beidh trácht air,
Nuair a throid na sárfhir go cróga tréan,
In aghaidh namhad go dána d'fhonn saoirse a thárlamh,
Is a bheith gan spleáchas ina dtír cheart féin.

[The story of Easter Week will be forever mentioned
When great men fought bravely adn stoutly
Against the enemy to attain freedom
And to be withoug dependence in their own rightful country.]

On the Kerry side of the border, Joe Dinneen was a well-loved poet who died in a train accident at Headford in 1929 and whose verse is still quoted. A brother of An tAthair Pádraig Ua Duinnín, he wrote on a huge array of subjects and could compose on request. Some of his poems, elegies in particular, and a number of extracts can be found in the *Sliabh Luachra Journal* and other local history publications. He has been portrayed as a poet in the old bardic tradition, the only difference being that he didn't enjoy the patronage that was accorded his predecessors.

In a profile of Joe Dinneen in the first issue of the *Sliabh Luachra Journal* (1982), John O'Mahony wrote that he was a chronicler of events and an entertainer of the masses in poems of simple words and elegant rhyme: 'His was the gift to express what others were thinking, to use his gift of words to articulate the thoughts that struggled for expression in less gifted minds.'

A speciality was his composition of 'Skelligs Lists' of folk who didn't marry by the old Shrove Tuesday deadline. (The monks on the Great Skellig island off the south Kerry coast had a very old way of calculating Easter, which could make their Easter – and consequently their Lent – as much as a few weeks later than on the mainland, and extend the window of opportunity for those wishing to marry during Shrove.) O'Mahony never lost hope for those meriting his attention:

John Dan Jack we won't let back, although he is but a pet,
He is the first and not the worst to give the boys a wet,
Miss Buckley fair, abiding near, controls his senses now,
He'll bring her home, she'll be his own, in gold-crowned Moulagow.

In the occasional home around the area, framed, black-bordered copies of Joe Dinneen's elegies still hang, such as his tribute to mark the first anniversary of the death of Cornelius O'Callaghan, of Gneeveguilla, in January 1902, sympathetically addressed to Miss Abina O'Callaghan:

Sad memory is recalling one year ago today,
When Con Callaghan was summoned from this vale of woes away;
Beneath yon polished marble his lifeless corpse now lies,
Which summons forth my genius to sing his obsequies.

Dinneen received a good education and studied a while for the priesthood. By all accounts he could write a poem at the proverbial drop of a hat. While his poetic output was prolific and some of his lines are remembered to this day, he sacrificed quantity for quality, according to John O'Mahony: 'He rarely spent time in revision and improvement, words seemed to take precedence over ideas, a criticism he shares with the great Eoghan Rua.' A book of his plays and poems was published in 1896.

A coeval of Joe's was Ned Buckley, a highly political poet from Knocknagree who had memorable exchanges in words with Seán Moylan, thc freedom fighter turned Fianna Fáil politician and cabinet minister to whom he was politically opposed. A self-educated man, he had a liking for the plays of William Shakespeare. Born in 1880, Buckley claimed descent from the Ó Scannail poets, of Meenagisheach, and his verse frequently appeared in publications such as the *Cork Weekly Examiner*. A book of his poems has also been published.

Buckley worked as a farm labourer, shoemaker and small shopkeeper and his home was a rambling house in Knocknagree, with subjects of conversation often providing material for his poems. Ned, who died in 1954, is also remembered as an orator who made political speeches on fair days and other public occasions.

He once wrote a parody of a Republican song, 'The Foggy Dew', in which he attacked the government of the day for doubling the dog licence fee. Called 'The Doggie Due', it went like this:

The licence for our Black and Tan
Was only half-a-crown

When work was sure and cash secure
In country and in town.
Now to keep their posts of Ministers,
Who have nought else to do,
In each fine job they ruled five bob
Should now be the Doggie Due.

There were many other local poets, including some of recent vintage such as Den Lynch of Rathmore, and John O'Mahony of Gneeveguilla. As well as writing verse, their versatility has also been called upon for the writing of scripts for local variety shows.

Of the younger generation, Eugene O'Connell from Kiskeam continues to establish his reputation as a poet and literary critic.[3] Like most of the others, he draws from the fountain of his own experiences and his native place. Poet and Trinity College professor Brendan Kennelly has described O'Connell's poems as being at once thoughtful and dramatic, adding that the poet himself is a sharp observer of people and places and a keen listener.

A common theme is emigration, and O'Connell's poem, 'Coming Home', pictures the scene when his aunt returned from New York after thirty-five years and was reunited with her mother.

Aged and worn she embraced
her newer daughter fresh
from dark Manhattan streets.

and numbered all those years
five and thirty since first she left.
And arm in arm together
they went into the house.
The dark kettle there
Humming their happy praises on the crane.

The exile's longing for home is also expressed by the aforementioned Dan Sheahan, of Newmarket, who though best remembered for 'A Pub with No Beer' also versified about his early years around Newmarket and Meelin before emigrating to Australia in 1905. In the energy-sapping heat of summers down under, he wistfully recalled former nights in Florrie Shea's pub in Newmarket:

I've wined and dined in flash saloons,
I've drank with Yanks and Yids and Coons –
I've sampled sly grog in a tent
And stayed there 'till my cash was spent.
Then sick and sore 'mid heat and haze
I wished I was at Florrie Shea's. 4

Dan toiled in the bush and also fought in France with the Australian army in World War I, commiting many of his experiences to verse. He composed 'A Pub with No Beer' on a summer's day in 1944 after calling to his favourite hostelry in Ingham, North Queensland, to slake his thirst. But war-time conditions had curtailed supplies and he was obviously upset to find that the pub had no brew. The poem was published in a local newspaper and was later slightly amended for recording as a song which was a hit and which is played on radio to this day.

It was a song that brought Dan more fame than fortune for he made no money out of it. This didn't trouble him. Instead he took satisfaction from the acclaim the song won and wished those using it all the best. Dan was an important figure in North Queensland, becoming involved in politics and the affairs of the area. He lived to the grand old age of ninety-four and died in 1977.

Finally, the aptly-dubbed Castleisland colossus, Con Houlihan, has to figure amongst the literati. He's not a poet in the strict sense, but his exquisite prose is as near as you'll get to poetry and he is a man in the tradition of the poets. Con is everyman's writer, being an essayist, columnist, journalist, wit, critic and a verbal stylist with a uniquely personal way of captivating readers.

His contributions to the now defunct *Evening Press* have been printed in book form more than once. Essays rather than mere columns, they cover subjects as diverse as evenings in pubs, the craic in Camden Town, Van Gogh, boxer and playboy Jack Doyle and memories of the broadcaster Micheal O'Hehir. His compulsive literary journey over the past half century also takes in Sliabh Luachra, with memorable notes about his days as a turf-cutter and potato-picker and as a young fellow winkling trout from streams around his birthplace.

The shy giant with the long mane of wispy, grey hair has earned a very special place for himself in Irish writing and in the affections of many people who, but for him, might never read a book, or paper. His output is quite astonishing and it will be some time before a proper assessment can be made of him and his work. Anyway, as he might say himself, he's too young yet.

He's at his best when describing the everyday lives and passions of both rural and urban folk. He has an extraordinary gift for telling about his youth around Castleisland as the following extract from one of his stories in the *Evening Press* about digging spuds with a neighbour, Tom Broder, in a field beneath fabled Gleannsharoon, illustrates:

> It was a lovely calm day; you could hear a leaf fall – or at least you imagined that you could; we worked at a fair rate of knots and got the job done. I remember vividly how beautiful the Kerr's Pinks looked in the low light of evening; the Golden Wonders were less colourful but had a beauty of their own.
>
> The blackbirds and the thrushes supplied the background music; about an hour before dusk a robin announced his presence.
>
> Not everyone is aware that a robin can sing; he is a brilliant musician with a great range and amazing power.

Some people may be inclined to believe that the songwriter took poetic licence when he wrote about the thrush and the robin entwining their sweet notes – they do . . .

There was one thing lacking on that October day long ago when we dug out Tom Broder's spuds; the field was a long way from any house – and so we had no hens to accompany us.

Hens love the digging of potatoes; it provides them with a bonanza. You will always find the best worms in potato ground – they are as caviar to the hens.[5]

Epilogue

Even though traditional Irish music enjoys continuing popularity, some people are deeply concerned for the future of distinct regional styles. A bit like the gradual demise of regional accents, music is also suffering from the rush to standardisation and the notion in some quarters that people should all play the same way. The growth of the recording industry and radio and television is contributing to this, not to mention music competitions which are judged on a 'national' standard.

Jack Roche of Rockchapel has been involved all his life in promoting the music and culture of Sliabh Luachra and he believes that while the music is not under threat, regional styles are in serious danger of disappearing.

Other enthusiasts, such as Dan O'Connell of Knocknagree, disagree, pointing out that hundreds of young people in Sliabh Luachra are learning the music and will keep it alive. Sharing O'Connell's view, Johnny O'Leary even argues that Sliabh Luachra music is spreading outside the area and winning new practitioners in other places.

Roche, a purist, an unapologetic traditionalist and a man of strong views and independent mind, is critical of musicians who in his words 'joyride' the Sliabh Luachra music by changing and adapting it for strictly commercial purposes. He is also sceptical of those who argue in favour of music evolving. 'The question is: where is evolution going to stop? People can take it to any lengths they like and maybe end up with something like bluegrass music.'

As he sees it, the dominant current trends are towards a cosmopolitan style of Irish music. He maintains that competitions and to a certain extent fleadhanna cheoil have contributed, claiming that anyone hoping to win a prize at a fleadh would have to change from a regional style. The swing towards a unified type of national music is also evident at sessions and fleadhanna where twenty or thirty reels make up most of the repertoire: more of a focus on rhythm to the detriment of melody. Roche exempts an t-Oireachtas from his criticism in relation to the downplaying of regional styles and says he would have higher regard for one prize won at the Oireachtas than several at a fleadh.

There are mixed views on the role of CCÉ. The organisation has undoubtedly been a major force in the revival and promotion of Irish music. On the other hand, it is criticised for an over-emphasis on competition and for undermining regional styles.

The Rockchapel CCÉ branch, of which Jack Roche is chairman, is a busy one. Its young musicians have travelled to Northern Ireland, Belgium, France and Scotland and they make a point of telling the story behind a tune, or a dance, thereby helping an audience to appreciate what they're doing. Two of their tunes – 'Allistrim's March' and 'Allistrim's Jig' – date back to the Battle of Cnoc na nOs, near Kanturk, in which General Allistrim fought in 1647.

Roche is currently trying to establish a core group from the young Rockchapel musicians (taught by Nicky McAuliffe) which will concentrate on the Sliabh Luachra style.

A regular visitor to the Rockchapel area is a young Dublin fiddler, Caoimhín Ó Raghallaigh, who came across the recorded music of Denis Murphy whilst working in the Traditional Music Archive. In June 1999 he launched a CD on the occasion of the official opening of Bruach na Carraige, a new cultural centre in Rockchapel, by President Mary McAleese. The CD, called *Turas go Tír na nÓg*, contains several Sliabh Luachra tunes and Ó Raghallaigh, who has no ancestral connections with the area, plays uncannily like Denis Murphy. As they say, he has the *draíocht*.

The maple-floored Bruach na Carraige, which cost £120,000 to build, is a splendid facility with an auditorium capable of seating more than a hundred people as well an archive room. It doesn't have a stage: instead, musicians sit by an open fire with the audience gathered round them.

A similar cultural centre is also under construction in Scartaglen.

Irony of the ironies is that while some EU policies

are forcing the people out of Sliabh Luachra and thereby undermining the culture, others are helping to preserve the culture – such as the LEADER programme, which has helped fund the two above-mentioned cultural centres.

Jack Roche is hopeful that there will at some time in the future be a return to regional styles, but stresses that time is not on the side of the regions. 'At least this generation knows that the music has been changed. The next generation may not. When the older Sliabh Luachra musicians pass on, it looks as if there won't be anyone to take their place. That's the big danger,' he cautions.

Ciarán Mac Mathúna is more optimistic. In his view the regional styles are still strong and people are again coming to realise how important it is to have such a variety of styles throughout the country.

Collectors such as Ballydesmond musician Dan Herlihy are also playing a critical role in gathering and collating many of the old tunes which are at risk of being lost forever. Musicians like Paddy Cronin are most concerned about fiddle-playing. They maintain that there's too much emphasis on the accordeon and argue that the fiddle can't be beaten for Sliabh Luachra music.

Accordeonist Denis Doody, a native of Ballydesmond who has lived in Shannon, County Clare, for many years, maintains that fiddle-playing in the style of O'Keeffe and Denis Murphy has virtually disappeared in Sliabh Luachra. These days Doody is invited to give talks on the music and all it entails at summer schools and university gatherings. He always identifies himself as being in the Sliabh Luachra tradition, but points out subtly that there are 'musicians from Sliabh Luachra and Sliabh Luachra musicians' – different species entirely.

Raymond O'Sullivan of Newmarket believes that the music is in a state of transition, coming from the house dance era into the pub and concert scene.

> The music must find a new level in the 21st century. There's a danger that musicians are beginning to leave the people and are no longer part of the people. We could be approaching the day where you'll have to pay to go into big halls to hear traditional musicians. That scene would be a huge break way from the traditional social background of the music in which a musician came from the people and was always one of them in everyday life in a locality.

He points to a situation where young musicians are geared for competitions and have 'barrels of medals' to prove their successes. But unlike their predecessors they couldn't play for a house dance. The music, he emphasises, must find its feet again – there's no going back to the days of crossroads dancing but the music must find a forum for itself in the modern world.

At one time, the scene was much more inclusive,

with attention always being given to singers. But this is no longer true and singers, with a few exceptions, find themselves being pushed to the margins – to the extent that singers now form their own unofficial clubs and find their own pubs in places like Castleisland and Knocknagree.

Just like singers, poets and songwriters are not as plentiful as they once were in the area. And no longer will you find men standing knee-deep in rushes reciting elegies or other works of Eoghan Rua. But poems – which nearly always become songs – are still composed to mark important events such as sporting or political victories.

As long as poems and songs are written there will be people to sing them and, regardless of the pervasive power of mass culture, the singing tradition has not entirely waned in Sliabh Luachra. The man or woman who can sing well can still command an appreciative audience in a pub or community hall. People may not be prepared to listen to singers all night, but the occasional song is always acceptable.

Recitations of poems are also generally welcomed as a novelty, but are not heard as often as formerly.

The drift of people from rural areas has been accelerated in recent years by EU agriculture policies which have made many of the small farms in Sliabh Luachra unviable. This, too, is having an effect on the culture of the area. Large-scale afforestation – particularly noticeable in the highland area between the Feale and the Blackwater – means that trees are replacing people. Small farms on which families were reared for generations are being sold off at an alarming rate. Bigger farmers are buying these farms, chiefly for the accompanying milk quotas, and are then planting the land. Huge tracts of countryside are being covered by trees.

As people leave, a way of life in Sliabh Luachra goes with them. As houses become scarcer, neighbourliness and a sense of sharing become almost irrelevant. The people have also been noted for their love of animals. Up to present times there were farms on which each cow had her own pet name, for instance, and people would stay up night after night with a cow expected to calve. All that is vanishing now and you're more likely to find very large herds of anonymous cows with half their tails gone and numbers branded on their rumps.

We hear lots of talk about cultural tourism and Sliabh Luachra is still a virgin area as far as this phenomenon is concerned. Tourism may have a future in the area, but locals don't want crowds of visitors descending on them. For starters, many of the roads in the area are not suitable for buses and the most interesting landmarks are often at the end of twisting, pot-holed bohereens.

However, people who are genuinely interested in the history and culture of Sliabh Luachra are always assured of a welcome and the area has much to offer the person who is looking for a no-frills, down-to-earth experience amongst naturally hospitable people. Selectivity may be the operative word here.

Some villages in the area hold annual fleadhanna cheoil, with the Scartaglen féile now being successfully staged for over thirty years. The Pádraig O'Keeffe Memorial Festival is an annual fixure in Castleisland. Impromptu music sessions can happen anywhere any time. One of the best events – the Denis Murphy Memorial Weekend held in Knocknagree in June each year – is in danger of becoming a victim of its own popularity. Indeed, this occasion is supposed to be a secret and the organisers have given up advertising it for the simple reason that the village is hard put to cope with the crowds that are sure to come. Crossroads dancing and, to a lesser extent, the rambling house tradition are also undergoing a little revival in parts of Sliabh Luachra and surrounding areas.

Set dancing is helping to keep the music alive, but there are people who just want to dance without necessarily having an interest in the music itself. Set dancing has been described as a timeless expression of joy and it shows no signs of decline, with teachers such as Timmy 'The Brit' McCarthy working wonders. Timmy rarely learns a dance from someone under the age of seventy and he's impressed with the degree of fitness shown by these light-stepping pensioners.

Respecting tradition, Timmy always names the person who gave him a particular dance and when he got it from them. He identifies dances with places: an expert can usually tell where a person comes from by the way he or she dances.

There's the story of an oldish lady who used to come to Timmy's classes. Her legs were a bit stiff, he observed, but she could dance with her eyebrows!

The undying spirit of Sliabh Luachra.

Notes

Chapter 1

1. Pádraig Ua Duinnín. 'Sliabh Luachra. Cá bhfuil Sé?' *Journal of Cumann Luachra*, Vol. 1, No. 1, 1982.
2. Charles Smith. *The Ancient and Present State of the County of Kerry*. First published 1756. Reprinted by Mercier Press 1969.
3. Dan Cronin. 'The City of Kerry's Kingdom'. *Journal of Cumann Luachra*, Vol. 1, No. 1, 1982.

Chapter 2

1. Interview with the author, January 1995.
2. *Journal of Cumann Luachra*, Vol 1 No 1, 1982. Each of the nine issues of the journal published to date contains at least one article on the music, or musicians.
3. Breandán Breathnach, *Folk Music and Dances of Ireland*, Mercier Press, 1971. (This is critically regarded as an excellent work on Irish music.)

Chapter 3

1. Article by Ray Ryan in the *Kerryman*, May 1969.
2. The volumes comprise a huge amount of detailed information including reprints of rare books and manuscripts, parish records, collections of poems,

ancient surveys and genealogical material containing up to three million personal names. They were published in 1952 in collaboration with T. E. Dowling.

3. Denis Spillane,'The Big Flood in Clydagh Valley', *Seanchas Dúthalla* (Duhallow Magazine) 1980–81.
4. For further information on the moving bog see *Journal of Cumann Luachra*, Vols. 1, 8 and 9.
5. Full account by Pádraig Ua Duinnín in *Journal of Cumann Luachra*, Vols. 1 and 2.

CHAPTER 4

1. From material sent by Éamon Kelly to author in 1994. See also first part of Éamon Kelly's autobiography, *The Apprentice*, Marino Books, 1995.

CHAPTER 5

1. Jim Thady Willie O'Connor, RIP.
2. For further information see Seán O Céilleachair's well-researched article, 'Going to the Hall', *Journal of Cumann Luachra*, Vol. 1, No. 4, 1987.
3. Richie Leader, Ballydesmond, who danced in the hall.
4. Interview with Jimmy O'Brien, Killarney.

CHAPTER 6

1. Éamon Kelly, *The Apprentice*, Marino Books, 1995.
2. See the second volume of Eamon Kelly's autobiography, *The Journeyman* (Marino Books, 1998), which tells of his professional life, first as a woodwork teacher and then as an actor.

CHAPTER 7

1. Catherine Murphy, *Treoir*, Uimhir 6, 1980.
2. Breandán Breathnach, *Ceol Rince na hEireann*, 1976.
3. *Treoir*, Uimhir 6, 1980.

CHAPTER 8

1. Terence 'Cuz' Teahan (with Josh Dunson), *The Road to Glountane*, Chicago, 1980.
2. Pádraig Ua Duinnín, 'Glimpses of Pádraig Ó Caoimh, *Journal of Cumann Luachra*, Vol 1. No 7, 1993.
3. *The Sliabh Luachra Fiddle Master Pádraig O'Keeffe* (CD, 1994).
4. Pádraig Ua Duinnín, *op. cit.*
5. *The Sliabh Luachra Fiddle Master Pádraig O'Keeffe* (as told by Timmy Browne), RTÉ programme produced by Peter Browne in 1994.

CHAPTER 9

1. The *Irish Press*, April 1974.
2. RTÉ radio programme (part two) on Denis Murphy produced and presented by Peter Browne in 1994 to co-incide with the launch of a cassette/CD of Denis Murphy's music.
3. *Ibid.*

CHAPTER 10

1. *Johnny O'Leary of Sliabh Luachra* (Lilliput Press, 1994), features some of the musician's old tunes which were collected by Terry Moylan and the late Breandán

Breathnach. An invaluable source of music for those interested in quintessential Sliabh Luachra material.

2. Johnny O'Leary, 'My Life and Music', *Journal of Cumann Luachra*, Vol. 1 No. 1, 1982

CHAPTER 11

1. For further details see article, 'My Life and Music', by Christy Cronin, *Journal of Cumann Luachra*, Vol. 1, No 5, June 1989.
2. Article in the *Kerryman* by Breda Joy, 10 April 1987.

CHAPTER 12

1. Séamus Ennis writing in *Treoir* magazine 1970.
2. Ciarán Mac Mathúna interview with author in Knocknagree, October 1994.
3. Peter Browne's *The Sliabh Luachra Fiddle Master Pádraig O'Keeffe* and *Denis Murphy – Music from Sliabh Luachra*, illustrated notes published in conjunction with the cassettes/CDs, 1993 and 1994, respectively.

CHAPTER 14

1. Mikey Duggan, 'My Life and Music', *Journal of Cumann Luachra*, Vol. 1, No 2, 1983.

CHAPTER 15

1. *Journal of Cumann Luachra*, Vol 1, No 4, June 1987.
2. It is still possible to find copies of the published collection of Ned Buckley's poems in the Sliabh Luachra and Duhallow areas. Joe Dinneen's collection,

Poems and Plays by Joe Dinneen, which was published in Tralee over a century ago, is now a rarity. In many houses, however, you will find copies of poems by both men – usually in the form of newspaper clippings or single broadsheets. Poems by Buckley and Dinneen are also to be found in local historical journals published in recent times.

CHAPTER 16

1. Fr P. S. Dinneen, *Four Notable Kerry Poets*, Dublin, Gill and Sons, 1929.
2. Daniel Corkery, *The Hidden Ireland* , Dublin, Gill and Sons, 1924.
3. *Ibid.*
4. *Ibid.*

CHAPTER 17

1. Con Houlihan, 'Tributaries', *Evening Press*, 1983.
2. *Amhráin Eoghain Ruaidh Uí Súilleabháin*, edited by An tAthair P. S. Ua Duinnín, Cumann na dTéacsleabhar Gaeilge, 1907.
3. Daniel Corkery, *The Hidden Ireland*, 1924.
4. Seán Ó Donnchú, 'The Hectic Life and Times of Eoghan Rua Ó Súilleabháin', *Journal of Cumann Luachra,* Vol. 1, No 1, 1982.
5. An t-Athair P. S. Ua Duinnin, *Four Notable Kerry Poets*, Dublin, 1929.

6. Tadhg Ua Duinnín,'Eoghan an Bhéil Bhinn – an Appreciation of His Poetry',*Journal of Cumann Luachra*, Vol. 1, No 2, 1983.
7. Dan Cronin.

CHAPTER 18

1. Prionsias Ó Conluain and Donncha Ó Ceilleachair, *An Duinnîneach*, a biography of Fr Dinneen. First published by Sairséal agus Dill, 1958. Essential reading for those interested in Fr Dinneen.
2. Quoted in Ó Conluain and Ó Céilleachair from *Lectures on the Irish Language Movement*, published by Muintir Ghoill, 1904.
3. Sceilg, Obituary for Fr Dinneen in the *Kerryman*, October 1934.

CHAPTER 20

1. Ray Ryan, Profile of Bernard O'Donoghue, the *Examiner*, 4 January 1996.
2. See *A North Cork Anthology* by Jack Lane and Brendan Clifford, Aubane Historical Society, 1993
3. See *Chapters of Little Times*, a collection of O'Connell's poems published by himself in Cork in 1995.
4. Miscellany by John Joe Brosnan, the *Corkman*, 18 May 1984.
5. For further helpings of Con Houlihan, a collection of his essays, *Windfalls*, published by Boglark Press in 1996, is highly recommended.

INDEX